The Circle Organization Novellas and Short Story

The Circle Series

Carla Swafford

Preface

Dear Reader,

Though the two novellas, Circle of Dishonor and Circle of Defiance, are standalones, as are The Circle novels, I suggest reading the full novels first to enjoy the short stories even more.

The suggested reading order with main characters follows.

- Circle of Desire (Olivia & Collin)
- Circle of Danger (Marie & Ryker)
- Circle of Deception (Abby & Rex)
- Circle of Dishonor (Lena & John)
- Circle of Defiance (Katerina & Jack)
- Kidnapped For A Day (Luke & Emma)

The events in the novellas happened after the novels. Jack appears in all of the novels as a secondary character, and the same for John (Ice) in the last two. Katerina made an appearance, but no dialogue, in the second book, though there was a secret appearance in the third book. If you read Circle of Deception, can you guess?

Thanks.

Carla

Circle of Dishonor

Chapter One

Lena Matthews felt like a perverted voyeur.

Sitting in a coffee shop across the courtyard from the martial arts studio's glass storefront, she stared at the tae kwon do class as they kicked and jabbed. Most of the students wore white pajama-like uniforms, except for the teacher. He stood out in black with his shaggy dark hair and ripped body. The man looked good enough to lick.

For the last five weeks after her tai chi class, she'd claimed the same chair and watched his every move. Behind her, others in the coffee shop chatted about the class and the mysterious man leading it.

From what she'd overhead, his name was John Takahashi, and the students called him Master J.

Master? Oh, yeah. She could imagine he'd master many things. With his strong hands and long muscled arms and legs, he likely controlled any situation or person. He could easily lift her and hold her against the wall as he stroked her to a climax. She whimpered and squeezed her knees together.

A shake of her head knocked out the dirty thoughts racing through her mind. She knew better. He'd never be attracted to an ordinary person like her. The woman he chose would be totally the opposite of her: young, athletic with honey blonde hair. Lena was about as interesting as watching bread turn to toast.

The rumors flying around in the coffee shop about Master J bounced from his being a former Japanese mobster to a government-sanctioned assassin assigned to a secret organization. First, from what she'd seen, there wasn't a tattoo on that fit body, and didn't all yakuza believe more was better? And second, how secret would the organization be if so many people knew of it? Everything sounded so farfetched. No one knew for sure what he did before opening up the studio, and he apparently refused to talk about his past.

The gossip fed her steamy fantasies of Master J, and she'd watched every Asian action film she could find on Netflix. She'd never been so infatuated with a stranger.

She smiled. It was amazing the things a person heard while pretending to be engrossed with the computer, but it fueled her imagination. She loved watching him. He certainly didn't have a problem with coordination. Every kick and twist was fluid, like poetry in motion.

In her absorption, she had to remember to occasionally look down at the computer so no one caught her gawking. Did it really matter what other people thought? So what if he was younger? What was the harm in watching? She was single again. It was healthy to look at men. Another peek across the courtyard and she breathed in deep. The man punched and jumped in the air as he strode gracefully across the studio.

Hello, mid-life crisis?

She felt like a sex-starved groupie drooling over the most exotic and probably dangerous man she'd ever seen. It didn't help that the last two weeks, halfway through the class, he always pulled off his shirt. Sweat looked good on his well-defined chest and abs, and the loose black pants he wore rode low, showing off his seriously cut body. He probably needed to be in shape to survive his world, if any of the rumors were true. A place she never thought a whole lot about before.

At that moment, the object of her obsession picked up a towel and wiped sweat from his face. When his eyes opened above the white cloth, their gazes met.

Oh, my God! She looked down and pretended to type. *Keep cool. He'll think it was a coincidence that I made eye contact.*

Her face flushed. The man wasn't dumb. He'd caught her doing the same thing last week. Would he think it an amusing fluke? Again?

Making a decision to run for it, she grabbed her satchel and stuffed in her laptop. She walked toward the door, staring at the floor and avoiding any chance of eye contact. What was she thinking, spying on him? The man was gorgeous, but so much younger and so out of her depth.

As soon as she stepped outside, head still down, she ran into something solid. A person.

Bare masculine toes wiggled an inch from her sneakers and warned of who stood there. How could bare feet be sexy? The desire to run quickly dissipated. She was no coward. She looked up. Master J stood in front of her with his black eyebrows raised, towel around his neck and shirt on.

Shirt on. Thank you, God, for small favors.

A brief smile crossed his face.

"Do I know you?" he asked with a slight Southern drawl.

So not what she thought he would sound like, but she liked it nevertheless.

Mortified by the confrontation but determined not to appear more foolish—she possessed some common sense—Lena straightened and looked into his dark eyes.

"No, but...I...I enjoy watching you teach your class... uh...I mean I enjoy watching your class." Her face heated. Oh, hell, when did she develop a speech impediment? *Pull yourself together, girl. He's just a guy like a lot of other guys, with muscles and gorgeous dark eyes that twinkle.* Who was she kidding? How often did she meet a man like him? All intimidating and lethal to her body and heart.

He dipped his head, hiding his amusement. "I'm honored."

She copied his action and then said, "If you will excuse me, I need to head home."

He caught her arm, his fingers gentle.

"Come. Have a cup of coffee with me."

"I don't drink coffee." She squeezed her eyes shut. That sounded so stupid though it was true. Why wouldn't he assume she drank the stuff? He'd caught her staring at him from a coffee shop, for goodness' sakes. "I mean, I prefer tea." When she opened her eyes, his grin grew bigger. He had a beautiful smile.

"Tea, then. I'll appreciate hearing about your opinion of my class. So we'll meet in five minutes?" He waited for her reply.

How could she turn him down? After weeks of obsessing over his looks and possible bad-boy past, there was only one answer. "Yes. I'd like that."

"I'll see you inside, then." He bowed his head and loped back across the open mall area.

That was when she noticed his class standing and watching from the martial arts school's large window. She covered her mouth, face flushed, and walked stiffly into the shop. Luckily, her table was still open, but this time she sat with her back to the view.

Was she foolish to think he could be interested in her? An older woman? Keeping her head and not going off the deep end thinking she was irresistible—*yeah, right*—she settled for the possibility he was merely curious about her.

Less than five minutes later, he strode over to her. His dark eyes never wavered from hers. He stopped at the chair across the table from her and asked, "Do you have a preference in tea?"

She looked up into his face. For the first time, she noticed the laugh lines that fanned away from his beautiful almond-shaped eyes. Maybe he was older than she thought. Her nerves calmed a little.

"Anything you like will be fine with me." She smiled. She didn't care why he decided to have tea with her. She only knew her body felt light and tight—happy with expectation.

"I hoped you'd say that." His gaze drifted from her face down her arms to her folded hands on the table. Had he checked for a wedding ring? He cleared his throat. "Excuse me. I haven't introduced myself. My name is John Takahashi."

"Yes. I know. I mean..." She sighed, frustrated. "I'm Lena Matthews. Nice to meet you."

She held out her hand to shake his. Instead, he clasped her fingers and bowed over them. His lips didn't touch her skin but tingles shot up her arm. Something so simple, yet she had to remember to breathe.

"Good to place a name with a lovely face." Before her blush deepened, he added, "I'll be back."

She watched as he threaded his way between the tables to the counter. Several heads turned as he passed. Even in loose clothes, his wide shoulders showed off his strength, and his confident walk dared anyone to stop him.

After he'd paid for two drinks and started back to her table, she looked down at her phone as if checking for messages, not that she ever had texts or emails. She wanted to make it look as if a good-looking man buying her tea was a daily, no-big-deal occurrence.

"Iced green tea will recharge you." He stripped the paper off a straw, speared it into the drink, and then slid it in front of her.

His kind gesture almost brought a sigh from her.

She sipped her tea. "Mmm, I needed that. Such warm weather for October."

"How do you like Richard Lee's tai chi class?" He tipped the glass as his unreadable gaze stayed on her face.

She'd picked tai chi as a way to get out of the house and exercise. Three years earlier, her husband, James, had died, leaving her plenty of money to retire young and enjoy life. The class had looked easy but she kept messing up the forms.

"Very nice. So relaxing." She cringed inside. *Such a silly lie.* Why not admit she was a klutz? And how did he know she'd been taking tai chi? Had he been watching her? That was a nice thought, that she had caught his attention too. Or had he been curious because he'd caught her staring before?

"Maybe our definitions of relaxing are different." He touched her arm, and she jumped. Then he sat back with a slight smile. His eyes twinkled again as he took another swallow of his tea, studying her over the glass. He appeared to be satisfied in proving she was strung tight as a virgin in the midst of male strippers.

Determined to change the direction of the awkward conversation, she asked, "How long have you practiced tae kwon do?"

His gaze drilled into her. "Since I was a child. Four years old."

"Oh, wow, that's so young."

"One of the tenets is self-control. A good ability to possess at any age."

"Do you teach other classes?" She sounded nosy, but he'd nearly finished his tea, and she wanted him to stay longer. Blast him! So far, he'd answered her questions and nothing more.

"No." Was that another smile he hid?

She searched her brain for a question that required him to give more than a one word answer. The desire to ask John about the rumors of his being a mobster or an assassin fought with her sensible side, but she had enough sense not to ask. "Where did you grow up? I detect a Southern accent. Texas?"

"Georgia. My mother was American and my dad was visiting from Japan."

Okay. Twelve words, and goodness, from his tone, he didn't like talking about himself. But in that little bit he'd told her a lot. His parents were not married. At least, that was her take on it.

He looked away and then returned his attention to her as he pushed back his chair and stood. "I'm sorry, but I have business to attend to. It was nice meeting you." He bowed his head slightly.

She hid her disappointment by smiling and picking up her satchel. Just because she found him fascinating didn't mean he felt the same in return. Her questioning obviously made him uncomfortable.

He followed her to the door and opened it. She adored his manners.

"It was nice meeting you too. Goodbye." The middle of her chest squeezed tight as she turned to walk to the parking deck. *Don't be silly, don't cry. No need to be so emotional.* He was only being nice to the crazy woman who'd been staring at him for the last few weeks.

Strong fingers grabbed hers and quickly let her go, a band of warmth lingered. She turned, forcing her smile to widen, determined to look unaffected by his indifference.

"If you're available tomorrow, I'd like to spend the evening with you," he said.

Spend the evening? She frowned. Did he mean a movie? Dinner? She loved the idea of spending more time with him. A date. It had been years. She wanted to hug his neck and cry at the same time. Thankfully, he was interested in more.

He added, "For dinner."

Smiling, she hugged the satchel to her chest. Trying to regain her voice as her emotions fought through a mixture of happiness and terror—he so out of her league—she lifted her gaze to his. He was so sexy. Her skin craved the feel of his sliding against hers.

Stop! You're getting ahead of yourself, Lena.

"That sounds lovely. I'd like that a lot." Did she sound overeager? Hell, she didn't care. She wanted this. It'd been three long years, and he was the first man to appeal to her in all that time.

"Good. I'll see you at eight." He headed in the opposite direction.

"Wait! You'll need my address and phone number." She blushed as several people frowned her way.

He looked back, and his gaze drifted over her. "I have them." Then he turned and strode out of sight into a small hallway between stores.

Her eyebrows lifted at his statement. Should she be concerned that he already had the information, or take it as a compliment that he had taken the time to look her up? For years, she and James ran their CPA business from a home office. Even though the business was closed for good, her information could be easily found. Truth be told, she'd Googled John but came up with at least a hundred hits on his name. None were about a man who taught martial arts and lived in Seattle.

A warm feeling pushed up the corners of her lips. He'd been interested enough to look her up. Nice. Then she remembered the heated look he'd given her before leaving. What had she gotten herself into?

<<<>>>

John Takahashi, also called Ice in the more deadly corners of the world, watched from the shadows as the woman slid into her Nissan Altima. He wanted to be certain she safely reached her car.

His hands tightened on the steering wheel.

A burly fellow strolled by Lena's car and continued to the next lane without glancing her way. John's hold eased up. If the man had attempted to attack her, bloody fat limbs would be scattered across the parking lot within seconds. He'd never allow anyone to harm her. Hell, if the man only spoke to her, John was unsure of his reaction. He'd never felt this way before. Possessiveness wasn't his usual response. He only knew she belonged to him.

From the first moment he saw her five weeks ago, intently watching him from the coffee shop, he'd decided to meet her. Her contradicting shyness and boldness amused him. The two times he'd allowed her to see him watching her, she'd looked away, blushing. He liked that. From the way she walked and held herself, he suspected she was a woman used to taking orders from a man. After being with so many women with that certain need, he had a sixth sense about such matters.

His contacts reported that her husband had died three years earlier. She wasn't a flirt and hadn't dated during that period. She dressed stylishly but modestly. Her hours were spent working in her house and in the flower beds surrounding her home. Occasionally, she had lunch with friends and attended charity functions, but nothing more.

Of course, their time in the coffee shop had been a test. If she'd been too timid or too bold, their time together would have ended without a dinner invitation. He wanted a woman willing to take commands but strong enough to demand what she needed in return.

As his gaze followed the taillights down the road, he adjusted his cock again. After years of working, practicing and conditioning his body, he never had a problem control-ling his responses. Until her. During the time he sat at the table, soaking in her shy demeanor, his cock had hardened and lengthened until he worried she would notice it even in his loose *dobok*.

Once he relaxed and regained control of his body he'd

left, lying to her about being needed elsewhere. It was only fair since she lied to him about her class. He'd spotted her first in the tai chi class. He'd watched her fumble the forms, stiff and uncomfortable with her body. Rather endearing. She only needed to learn how to relax, and he knew just the way to help her.

Chapter Two

Fidgeting with the blinds, Lena mentally slapped her own hand and turned away. She didn't want to appear anxious. Another glance at the clock brought a rush of excitement, only two minutes until eight. She was nervous. Her first date in over twenty years and as far as she knew, he could be a stalker.

How ironic. She'd stalked him by sitting at the coffee shop each week, sighing over his every move. Then she shamelessly eavesdropped whenever his name was mentioned nearby. She even Googled him again twice that morning. She still didn't know where he lived or his phone number. He was like a ghost. Maybe she should've listened harder to the rumors of his involvement in criminal activities.

It was time for her to stop worrying and take a chance and go with the sixth sense James had always claimed she possessed. He'd said she had a talent in distinguishing between the honest and the fraudulent clients. One thing was for certain: sitting across the table from John as he looked into her eyes, she'd felt warm and safe. Deep inside, she felt he had no plans to hurt her.

The crunch of gravel alerted her of a car coming into her cul-de-sac. A black sedan pulled to the curb and stopped near her mailbox, the headlights pointing out of the circle. She didn't recognize the make, but it looked no different from a thousand others on the streets. Well-maintained but nondescript like someone with the FBI or CIA would drive. A soft knock pulled her back to a more mundane world.

Hoping her plain black dress with white pearls was appropriate for where they were going, she opened the door.

She bit her bottom lip. Her first thought on eyeing his black suit, black tie and white shirt was the movie *Hitman,* but then John's tie should be red. Why had that crazy thought gone through her head? The wildest thing to ever happen to her was meeting the man she had a date with this evening.

Oh, but the simple colors suited him. His clothes were tailored and made from expensive fabric, showing off his broad shoulders and predator-lean build. Yes, she felt a clench in her stomach. The man was sex on a stick.

"You look so handsome." She bit her bottom lip again. Embarrassed by her bluntness, she sighed silently and forced a smile onto her face.

He grinned. "And I'm a fortunate man to have such a lovely woman on my arm tonight."

She loved the way he spoke, his choice of words almost poetic, and with his slight Southern accent they came across as old-fashioned.

"Would you like a drink?" She stepped back so he could enter.

"Thank you, no." He swept his arm toward his car. "Our reservations are at nine, and we have a distance to go."

"Okay." She picked up her shawl and then turned the lock before closing the door.

He leaned over and tested the knob. "You need a deadbolt too. It'll be safer."

"I meant to get one but keep forgetting to call. Thankfully, this neighborhood doesn't have trouble with break-ins."

"I'll have one put in for you tomorrow." He walked with her to the passenger door and opened it, waiting for her to slip inside.

"I can't let you do that," she said. He closed the door without responding. When he was behind the wheel, she added, "Really. We've just met and that would be too much." He remained quiet, only giving her a glance as he placed the car in gear. "At least, let me pay for his time and the lock."

"I offered, and it's no trouble." His even tone indicated he wasn't interested in further discussion.

She didn't want to start their first evening together in an argument, and besides, it was awfully kind of him, so she dropped the subject for now.

"Where's this restaurant you're taking me to?" She smoothed her dress over her knees. Her whole body felt as if bees buzzed under her skin in anticipation of the evening with a handsome man. It had been too long.

"It's on a small island with a beautiful view of the Puget Sound. They have the freshest seafood in all of Seattle." He glanced at her and then pushed a button. Immediately heat blasted near her feet. Her shawl had been a poor choice as it was cooler than she'd expected.

She liked how he looked after her. It'd been a long time since anyone treated her with such care.

"I love seafood, especially shrimp."

"Do you like opera?" he asked.

"I don't know much about it, but I enjoy listening to it."

"That's all that matters. I'm not much of a conversationalist while driving. So I hope you don't mind..." He turned a dial and the most soothing song filled the car. She leaned back into the soft leather seat to listen.

Taking advantage of his concentration on the wet roads, she soaked in everything she liked about him. His shaggy hair, dark eyes, cheekbones many women would die to possess, the broad shoulders she'd noticed earlier, and how his chest stretched the shirt in the right places. The more time she spent with John, the more she realized his cloak of maturity was not only experience but age too. Maybe he was in his late thirties.

"John?"

"Yes." He turned down the music.

"I know it's rude, but how old are you?"

"Thirty-nine as of last month."

Almost four years younger. Her birthday was the end of this month, and she'd be forty-three. Still that was better than when she suspected a ten-year difference. So much better.

He turned up the music without asking *her* age, or why she'd asked. She released her breath. Then she frowned. Wasn't he interested in getting to know her? Maybe he planned to wait until they reached the restaurant.

The warmth of his car and the beautiful music enveloped her as she leaned against the door, almost hypnotized by the passing scenery. Everything combined gave her the feeling of comfort and safety especially with such a conscientious driver. When the car came to a stop, she jumped. Please say that she hadn't fallen asleep and drooled.

"I'm so sorry. You should've nudged me awake. All I can say in my defense is that the last few days I haven't slept well."

"Lena, I like that you feel comfortable around me. Don't worry. Now I'll have your full attention." He brushed hair from her face.

Still embarrassed, she melted in her seat and smiled. Though he didn't return it, she sensed she pleased him. With what exactly, she wasn't certain, but she didn't care. She'd been thinking and dreaming about him the last few weeks, and she refused to let anything spoil their time together.

The restaurant had windows on three sides, giving the patrons plenty to look at, especially the view of the surrounding inlet. The smooth surface stretched for a good mile or more, and the way the building was angled, she felt as if the building floated on the water.

As the hostess led them to their seats, a nice looking man stood a few tables over and waved at John. "Takahashi, come and sit with us."

John lightly touched her arm. "Lena, I'm sorry, but they're old friends, and I must accept their invitation." He placed an arm around her waist.

"I understand. It'll be nice to meet friends of yours."

He grunted as if in approval and squeezed her to his side.

She'd meant it. Though she looked forward to talking with John one on one, friends were more apt to repeat stories that would show her layers of the man. Considering how quiet John had proven to be at this point, she hadn't counted on learning much about him tonight.

The striking auburn-haired woman sitting next to the handsome man frowned at John as if she couldn't place him and then switched her attention to Lena. The coldness in the woman's green eyes caused Lena to hesitate and only John's assuring touch helped her move forward.

"Lena, let me introduce you to Collin and his wife, Olivia. They run a local adoption agency. This is my special friend, Lena." John held out the chair for her next to the window, across from Olivia, and then he sat next to her across from Collin.

"Ice!" The woman blurted out and then turned to her husband, hitting his shoulder. "His hair isn't neon blue or long. I didn't recognize him."

"It has been a while," John said without looking at Lena. "I prefer John."

Ice? She could see someone calling him that. His calm manner probably came across to most as a cold disposition, but she saw the warmth underneath his self-control.

Collin rubbed his shoulder, giving his wife a heated glance, and asked, "How's your sister? Mai?"

"She's well. She returned to Japan and is married to a *salaryman*. Very happy."

She blinked and bit her tongue. Blue hair and a sister? Talk about an arsenal of questions she'd love to ask on the drive back home. But she didn't feel comfortable asking too many. She preferred he volunteered most of the information. Maybe on the next date.

Next date? Pushing it, wasn't she? She needed to concentrate on this one.

"Did you hear that Ryker and Marie had a baby? A little girl. They named her Margaret Olivia." Collin laughed.

"Can you believe it? I'm not only a mom and aunt but a godmother too. The world is a crazy place." Olivia shook her head and smiled. Despite the woman's hard exterior, her eyes softened when she talked about children.

The evening turned into a surreal time. Though she relished hearing about their attempts to match parents with orphans, she sensed there was a lot left out of the stories. But she could tell John tried his best to include her in the conversation by occasionally asking her opinion. The man was bossy. He'd ordered her meal without checking which shrimp meal she preferred. Yet, he demonstrated such attention and care toward her, she forgave him. She'd never have guessed she enjoyed being handled as if she needed a keeper.

He buttered a yeast roll and slipped it on the small plate near her. She glanced over and his hint of a smile shot warmth throughout her body. He could be her keeper anytime.

As the meal came to an end, everyone turned down dessert and coffee.

"How about coming to the house with us and having a drink?" Collin asked as they waited for the valet to bring their cars.

"Maybe another time," John said.

Lena looked away, not wanting them to see her relief. The couple appeared nice, but she sensed they were holding something back. She felt as if she was one beat off the rhythm. Besides she craved more time alone with John, even in the near silence of the car.

Lena shivered. She'd left her shawl in the sedan earlier,

not thinking about waiting outside for the valet. At that moment, warm material landed on her shoulders. John's knuckles brushed her neck as he pulled on the lapels. A different kind of shiver traveled across her skin. She looked up. His dark eyes stared deep into hers. She snuggled into the scent of John, sandalwood and man.

"Thank you," she said. Feeling a little awkward under the intensity of his gaze, she glanced over toward Olivia and caught the quizzical look the woman gave John. Besides the absence of long blue hair, had John changed a lot since the last time Olivia had known him? Lena understood how that could happen. She wasn't the same person she'd been with James.

From what little she'd gleaned from their conversations, they had worked together at one time. Though they never indicated in what capacity, from the couple's mannerisms, she would never want to meet them in a dark alley.

She shivered again.

Lena pulled the jacket tighter. The lapels almost touched the opposite arms, proving his shoulders were as wide as they had looked bare.

A black Maserati pulled up. The Rykers' adoption business must be successful.

She waved goodbye as the couple drove off and then she took a deep breath.

"They can be overwhelming." John smiled down at her as his sedan pulled up.

She smiled back and said before he closed the passenger door, "You're so right."

During the return drive, he was less intense and quiet. So different from the Rykers. Though, being truthful with herself, she liked John's calm manner. She knew he had layers she hadn't yet seen. She looked forward to learning more about him, if he would allow it. But so far, he hadn't shown any interest in another date.

Just because she found him interesting and different from anyone she'd ever met, didn't mean she appealed to him. What if she'd bored him to tears?

He shifted in his seat and looked over at her for a second before returning his attention to the road. "I hope you'll have dinner with me again tomorrow night," he said in a soft, deep tone.

Lena's heart picked up speed. It was as if he'd read her mind.

"I would like that."

"Good." His gaze remained ahead, and he didn't say anything more. She'd never been much of a talker, so his quietness didn't bother her.

She leaned back, unable to take her eyes off John. He was no more than a silhouette in the passing headlights. Time zoomed by and they arrived at her house before she wanted the night to end. As he strode alongside her to the small porch, his gaze swept the area as if he wanted to ensure that all was right and no one hid in the bushes. When they reached the stoop, she handed his jacket over and turned to unlock the door.

"So eight tomorrow?" she asked as she nudged the door open.

"How about six?"

Pleased that he was as anxious to see her as she was him, she gave him a big smile. A light feeling came over her.

"Yes. Tonight went by too fast." She hesitated. Would it be polite for her to kiss him on the cheek or would he think her too forward? What he thought about her was too important.

She silently sighed and then said, "Well, until then."

He cupped her cheek and leaned forward. His lips brushed the corner of her mouth. Then he pushed her door open wider and waited for her to enter.

She placed her fingers over where he'd kissed her and walked in without another word.

Before he closed the door, he said, "Lock the door. Tomorrow, wear something simple."

It wasn't until he drove away that she wondered what he meant. Maybe casual? Whatever. She couldn't wait. A new feeling came over her. She felt young and desirable for the first time in a long, long while. Strange considering he hadn't even given her a real kiss yet.

The black sedan sat with the motor running around the corner from Lena's house, but still in view. John questioned his reasons for watching her house. Presently, she wasn't in danger. None of his enemies knew about her. He'd taken precautions. Two of his men had stayed to keep an eye on the house, making sure no one messed with it.

He normally didn't play while on assignment, but he'd been unable to resist meeting her. Everything about her cried for his attention, for what only he could offer, and so far, he hadn't been disappointed.

She'd looked lovely tonight. Even in the dim light of the restaurant, her sable hair tempted him to sink his hands into the softness and hold her.

He lifted the shawl that she'd forgotten and smelled her delicate scent, a mixture of fresh air and vanilla. Her easygoing manner covered a tightly coiled need given away by every flick of her interested glances. He liked that.

His cock throbbed as he shifted the car into drive. Time for him to go home and prepare. He'd made the right decision. She was perfect and well worth the risk. He'd already waited several weeks. Tomorrow night wouldn't be too early. Lena was ripe for what he had planned.

Chapter Three

Lena dreamed about John, only it wasn't him. When his friend, Olivia, had mentioned he had long neon blue hair at one time, it had caught her interest, and she planned to ask him tomorrow night. Her subconscious obviously thought it fascinating too.

In her dream, John leaned over her. His long hair surrounded her face with different shades of bright blue. Dark eyes heated with desire stared down at her. She shivered as he appeared even more exotic and dangerous. He wore samurai armor. The iron and leather plates pressed against her naked body.

His bare hands lifted and squeezed her breasts, and she threw back her head and arched her torso to press harder. The low guttural words he said, she didn't understand, but she knew he told her what he planned to do to her. Yearning surged through her body. Moisture seeped between her legs. She craved what he promised.

His armor pinched and jabbed her tender skin with every movement he made against her. Yet, the pain intensified her desire for his possession.

Then he thrust into her, and she arched her back and moaned.

"Please!" she cried, wanting more, wanting it harder.

Her eyes opened. Every inch of her body hot, sweaty and wound tight in need, she groaned as she thrust fingers into the wetness between her legs. A couple strokes and she shook from the climax.

If she came from just dreaming about him, what would the real deal feel like?

<<<>>>

The next evening, she dressed in a simple navy blue sleeveless dress with a thick, short jacket and navy ballet slippers. She felt that was as casual as she could get in October. Normally, she wore jeans and a wool pullover, but she wanted to look feminine for him. Going from car to restaurant, she should be warm enough. Otherwise, it would be a wonderful reason to wear whatever jacket or coat he had on. She loved wearing his scent.

The knock echoed through her living room. She hadn't even heard the car pull up this time.

When she opened the door, his unfathomable gaze swept over her but then quickly heated. The look brought back the memory of the dream from the night before. She wanted to jump into his arms and kiss him. Restraint was one of her virtues that she wanted to leave behind tonight.

"Was this what you had in mind?" She twirled. She didn't want to embarrass him if she had misunderstood. He wore black slacks and a dark grey pullover sweater. Damn, he looked good in anything.

"Perfect." He stepped back to let her lock her door.

"And thank you for sending the man over to put in the

deadbolt. He not only took care of the front door, but the garage and back doors. I really wish you would let me pay for it. We've only had one date."

He shook his head. "We've had two dates. I count the coffee shop as the first."

Third date? Was he implying what she hoped? Hadn't she read in some women's magazine that it was okay to have sex on the third date? Doesn't matter. If he asked her, the new Lena Matthews would say yes. Hell, yeah, that was a given.

But how good would she be at it? James had often complained about her lack of passion in bed. What would an exotic man like John expect? Would she bore him too? She'd never been graceful or inventive, especially while naked and in bed. Maybe that was why she was willing to gamble with him. Other men she'd met had never tempted her to take a chance like he did. She admitted that the prospect of disappointing him scared her. Could she withstand his look of pity?

His hand pressed the small of her back. Heat shot through her body. Oh, my, how did he turn her on with such a simple touch? Was it worth risking humiliation?

"Where are we going this time?" she asked after regaining her wits.

He didn't say anything until she buckled the seatbelt, and he slipped behind the steering wheel. "I hope you don't mind, but I wanted to make sure there're no interruptions tonight. So we're going to eat at my house."

She guessed she should protest, but what was the difference? His house or hers. She looked at her home. No. She wanted adventure. Her curiosity won out. Where else could she learn more about him than at his place? Anyone who entered hers would learn she loved flowers from all the filled vases sitting around, and how much she loved to travel by the numerous pictures on her walls.

"That's a lovely idea." She turned toward him and gave him a big smile.

He gazed at her for a moment, his eyes halfway closed in approval. Then he shifted the car into drive.

For several miles they traveled on Interstate Five. After they exited, he turned several times—she felt like they were going in circles—until they turned off the road and stopped at a large ornamental metal gate with a small building next to it. A man in a suit similar to the one John wore the night before opened the gate and waved. As they drove through, Lena looked back. There were two more men, but instead of suits, they wore black combat gear and had what appeared to be rifles across their torsos.

"Uh, John. What kind of gated community is this?" She'd never seen such security before. Her hands smoothed the dress over her knees as her eyes scanned the area with growing alarm. What had she gotten herself into?

"Sorry. This is my property. I should've warned you. Because of the work I do, I'm required to use extra precautions. Don't worry. Everything is okay." He stopped the car and turned to her.

Was he part of the Japanese mob like so many speculated?

"We're safe. Trust me." He patted her hand. His dark eyes softened as he looked into hers.

His simple touch reassured her as much as his kind concern. She slumped back in her seat. Yes. She trusted him. Why? She wasn't sure but deep inside she knew he'd never harm her or let anyone else.

"All right."

He squeezed her hand and let go, placing the car back into gear.

Well, if nothing else, his undivided attention on the road was explained. If she had someone out to kill her, she'd never let her concentration drift elsewhere.

The lane continued on with a few well-placed streetlights, giving the blacktop a strange sheen. How long was the driveway? After what felt like a half mile, they passed another small neat building with two more guards on duty.

When they emerged from the trees, her mouth dropped open. The two-story house sitting on a side of a mountain was huge. Most of it was glass and she could see all the way through in some areas. How could such a cautious man live in a glass house?

"Bullet proof," he said as if he'd read her mind. Then he talked about the design of his home as he pulled up to one of six closed garage bays beneath the house.

She didn't understand much about what he said of how his home's interior panels opened and closed, providing the occupants privacy in the evening hours. From what she could see, it was beautiful, the lines clean and uncomplicated.

He pressed a button above the rearview mirror and a garage door lifted. Inside were several cars and a couple of motorcycles, not a one with a price ticket below a hundred thousand if she'd had to guess.

The only reason she recognized most of them was that her husband had always dreamed of owning a Bugatti or even a Rolls Royce. Yes, John was a man of contradictions who hid more than he revealed. For him to let her see all of this meant something, but she hadn't quite figured out what. She wanted to know more about how he ticked, what made him so protective of women. Or was it just her?

She felt safe with him.

How many times did she need to say that? Was she trying to convince herself?

As soon as they exited a small elevator, Lena gasped. The view from his living room was breathtaking. It framed the Cascades in the distance. The interior of the house was simple but luxurious. Lots of rice paper dividers he called *fusuma*, with designs of trees, mountains and birds, and a few plain ones that were outlined with black lacquer.

"Come. The food should be ready for us." He pulled a panel to the side and revealed an American-style oak table with napkins, glasses, and silverware and two cushioned chairs. Off to the side was a cart filled with silver-domed plates.

"Why do I have a feeling this was set up for me?" From what she'd seen of the house so far, the table and chairs were the only western furniture.

"For a woman to come to a man's house after knowing him for a short time and to see armed guards takes a lot of trust. The least I can do is to make you comfortable." He held out the chair until she sat.

Oh, goodness, how could a woman not melt?

He picked up a remote and the beautiful panels moved, blocking the front with the long winding drive, but allowing a view of a thick forest near the house. Strangely, a feeling of the world being locked out comforted her. It was just the two of them with no interruptions. Exactly what she wanted.

For the next thirty minutes or so, they ate and talked about the house, the weather and their favorite movies. All safe subjects until she finally asked him the questions she'd been dying to know since last night, though she worked at keeping the image of the blue-haired samurai from her mind.

"Your sister, is she older or younger?"

He leaned back in his chair and pressed a napkin to his lips for a moment as if to consider his answer. Maybe she'd stepped over the line. She hated being so uncertain.

"I'm sorry. If you'd rather not talk about family, that's okay," she said.

"No. I don't mind. The answer involves a sordid affair that I wasn't sure how best to explain. She's my younger half-sister. My father never married my American mother. He believed she was stupid and beneath him. Instead he shamed her and returned to his good Japanese family to marry the good Japanese woman they picked out for him. The two families are quite wealthy and traditional." He glanced out the window to the swaying trees. It had begun to rain. "I don't know why I told you that."

By the way he held his back straight, she could tell there was more to the story, but he remained silent. She'd been surprised he revealed as much as he did. A quick peek at his reflection in the glass showed the sadness mixed with anger crossing his face.

Not wanting to spoil the night, she changed the subject. "Tell me about the long blue hair and the nickname Ice." She smiled in an effort to place him at ease.

He remained stiff as he shook his head and said, "Yes, long and neon blue and another person and another lifetime ago. Let's move to the den where we'll be more comfortable." He walked around the table and pulled back the chair and placed her hand on his arm. "This way. I'll tell you about it after we have a glass of wine."

His evasive answer didn't bother her. He obviously detested talking about himself and hated that he said too much already. She understood. Everyone had regrets. How often after James died had people asked her an innocent question that caused her to slide into a defensive mode, her answer delivered with a smart-alecky mouth? Maybe it was tied in with her insecurity. She expected them to use the information against her. Her husband had done that often enough.

John's hand pressed the small of her back, leading her to a small balcony that looked over a large room. Again, American-style furniture, but in this case two sectional couches, one solid black and the other white. They had a slight Asian look with their simple design and close-to-the-floor profile. She imagined being stretched out on one of them with John on top. A flare of heat drifted over her skin, tightening the sensitive area around her nipples.

They walked down the wide staircase. Before her was a floor-to-ceiling window and on the other side a tall, thin waterfall fell from a steep incline into a lighted pool of water. She expected deer and fairies to show up. It was that magical.

Her attention returned to the room. On one wall a fireplace filled with logs burned brightly. A large furry black rug spread out in front of the fire. Soft music started playing. She looked around for the electronic equipment. It was well hidden.

Talk about a scene for seduction. He was proving to be an expert, and she was glad. Every inch of her sizzled with a need for his touch and to touch in turn. She was beyond ready. Her skin felt electrified.

He handed her a glass of white wine. "Let's sit over here." With a grace she envied, he stretched out on the rug.

He looked like sin incarnate sipping on a glass of wine.

She placed her glass on the floor and then eased down

beside him, but remained upright, too self-conscious to imitate him.

"Here. Let me help you with that coat before you get too warm," he offered.

At first, she thought he referred to the fire's heat, but from the way his gaze drifted to her breasts, she knew he talked about another kind of warmth. She unbuttoned her jacket without hesitation and handed it to him. He tossed it over the nearest sectional and pulled her into his arms.

Before she could say anything, he whispered, "Shh, just let me hold you. We have all night and more if you wish."

Her heartbeat picked up speed until she found it difficult to catch her breath. "I'm not sure. I—"

He sat up and placed a finger over her lips. "Enjoy the fireplace, we'll take it slow. If I do anything that makes you feel uncomfortable, tell me."

Unable to resist, she relaxed against him. As if she weighed nothing, and she knew better, he slid her around to face the fireplace and rested her head against his chest.

"Your husband...he hurt you," he said without doubt.

"You're crazy if you think I would ever let James hit me." She tried to sit up but he held onto her until she relaxed again. Oh, no, she didn't want to go there.

"Shh. There are many ways to wound a person." His hands skimmed up her arms. Suddenly the room became overheated. The flames jumped and flared, mimicking her desire for the man touching her to do more than talk.

She rubbed her cheek against the soft material of his shirt. Her eyes closed for a moment as she soaked in the pleasure of being held. How long had it been? Longer than James had been dead. Her husband had never been a fan of snuggling.

"True," she said, hoping he would drop the subject.

Being with him in such a romantic setting wasn't the place for sad tales, and she refused to be drawn into that dark pit. Was that how he felt when she asked him questions?

"Tell me."

How well she knew someone could dish out pain without lifting a hand. If she wanted answers from him, she needed to do the same in return.

"He never physically injured me. It's like this. A stranger's cruel words don't harm another, but when you love that person who speaks so callously, the pain goes deep and takes a long time to fade away."

She really didn't want to talk about her marriage. Since her husband's death she tried to think about only the good. No need to hash over something that was too late to change. The past could stay dead, and she was ready for a new future.

His hold tightened. Without a word he'd told her she had no fear of being treated in such a way by him. Hadn't she already reminded herself that she trusted him?

After a few moments of soaking in his acceptance of her explanation and gathering the courage, she decided to ask the one question uppermost in her mind.

"Do you work for the government as an assassin?"

John grinned against her hair. The little wren pretending to be a lion. He'd seen the fear in her eyes several times during their meeting in the coffee shop and at the restaurant and even this evening. The fear didn't have anything to do with what everyone speculated that he did for a living. No. She was afraid of being swept away by what he made her feel.

Chances were her husband had a hand in that fear too. Had he pressed old puritanical beliefs on a free bird? The woman in his arms wanted to let go and fly, enjoy sex and explore its many facets, but she was too afraid to take that final step off the ledge. She worried she'd never be the same. And she was right.

"John?"

"No. I don't work for the government." He grinned. Hearing the small catch in her breath, he knew she'd understood why he left out the last word of her question. She didn't move away. Maybe she could handle hearing the darkest part of his story.

His little bird needed an anchor. She needed to hear things about his life to feel like she made the right decision in coming here with him. He wasn't sure if he could give her everything she wanted, but he could give her that. "I work for an organization that deals with private security and investigations. Some of the missions are dangerous, and we associate with groups who would like nothing more than to kill us all."

"Why did you sign up with them?" She snuggled deeper into his arms. He looked down into her sweet face. Concern widened her big brown eyes. He slipped a hand over her shoulder and down to one breast. Beneath the material the hard tip teased the center of his palm.

"They taught me skills I needed."

"What skills?"

He hesitated and then said, "How to kill a man." He knew she was a woman who would keep his secrets.

Her body stiffened. "I really don't believe that's a skill."

Using one finger, he rubbed the hard nipple. Her breathing picked up speed. "It is if you wish not to be caught."

"Why are you telling me this? Do you want to frighten me?" Despite the words, she squeezed his arms tighter to her body.

"No. I just want you to know what type of man you came home with. I'll never harm a woman. But a man who destroys a woman's dignity and every reason for living, who laughs in her face when she begs him to stay, a man who ignores the reaching arms of his crying child as he walks out the door. That man deserves death."

"Your father?"

"Yes." He couldn't tell her yet of the depths he wallowed in to achieve his purpose of life. His father had known when he left the States that his son would find him again and bring retribution down on his head.

His mom rarely spoke of his father after that day. The dishonor of his abandonment slowly choked the life out of her. She worked menial jobs and struggled to place food on the table until John was old enough to help. He did anything for a buck. He joined a gang and became their collector, the one who pressed others to pay up on their protection money. After she died, he became a man possessed. He wanted vengeance. In the mercenary organization, The Circle, he increased his expertise in tae kwon do along with several other martial practices as well as firearms and explosives.

Every goal he set was for one purpose. When he reached twenty-five, he knew he was ready. So he flew to Japan and found the old man. His father was part of the *yakuza*, the Japanese mob, as their *shingiin*, law advisor. A position that guaranteed they would come after John. He didn't care. Once he returned to the U. S., he'd prepared for retaliation. In defiance, he grew his hair long and dyed it neon blue. He wanted to make sure they knew where to find him.

Then finally one day a message came. They wouldn't pursue the man they called *Koori*, Ice. Anyone who would dare walk into a meeting with a room full of *kyodai*, experienced *yakuza* soldiers, and kill his father without blinking an eye had a heart of ice and was most likely possessed by demons. That might not have been enough to save him if his father's involvement in embezzlement hadn't come to light soon after his funeral. John had saved the *yakuza* from having to execute the old man. His father had never known honor.

She twisted in his arms and looked into his eyes. He couldn't tell her any of that. Not yet. When her eyes welled up, he knew his face showed his pain. Then she did something he never expected. She cupped his cheek and pressed her lips to his. A closed kiss of comfort. He felt warm moisture on his face. He wrapped his hands in her hair and pulled her back enough to look into her eyes. Tears streamed down her cheeks.

"Why the tears?"

"He must've hurt you dearly."

"Nothing compared to how he destroyed my mother."

"But he destroyed a little boy's heart too."

Her eyes told him everything he needed to know. Though he hadn't told her the details, she understood he regretted the years wasted in his hate and plans for vengeance. And she was right. For years he'd believed he did it only for his mother, but he did it for himself too, for the five-year-old who cried for his father each night.

He leaned down and kissed her neck, savoring the taste of a real woman. Her moan vibrated through his soul. It wasn't until he held her in his arms that he realized his heart needed something to fill the emptiness. He needed a person to have faith in him, to believe he was a good person inside and deserved someone to hold and comfort him. And Lena did that beautifully as her hands slipped beneath his shirt and pressed his chest to hers.

<<<>>>

Lena's fingers dipped beneath his pullover and she moaned again with pleasure. Every hard muscle, every hollow and rise on his torso, she'd dreamed about touching him for weeks. It was so much better than her imagination. She lifted his top, pulling it over his head and off. The view was like she remembered but so much better up close and personal.

His arms circled her and the top of the sundress dropped to her waist. With the ease of an expert, he'd flipped the buttons at the back. A second later, he unhooked the last barrier to her bare breasts. He jerked her lacy bra away and tugged off her dress.

John still wore his slacks and his cock's length pressed against the material. She felt decadent being the only one naked. She savored it. His strong fingers pulled at her nipples, pushing her close to crying out in pleasure, and before she could catch her breath, his mouth covered a hard tip. Her fingers sank into his hair, holding his head. At the same time, the clicking of a zipper being lowered excited her beyond measure. He grasped her hands and gently untangled them from his hair.

She tried to open her eyes wider, but she felt drugged by the sensations controlling her body. In the flickering light, he leaned back and watched her as he tore open a familiar square package. Then he shifted, rolling on a condom. The man had a beautiful cock.

All of this was moving fast. He was moving fast. She struggled to breathe. Each intake and exhale filled her ears and surely echoed in the room.

She didn't want him to slow down. If he did, she would begin to worry about doing something wrong.

Her heart thumped against her chest and her legs trembled. Excitement swelled as she watched his fingers smooth the thin latex over his hard cock. She needed him now.

Her forehead wrinkled. They hadn't even kissed. Was she doing this right? Damn, she needed to quit worrying and let go. Let John lead the way. It had been so long since she felt this way. She never experienced such strong sexual magnetism, even with James. Was she letting her attraction control her common sense?

By the look on his face, her worry obviously showed.

He leaned over and cupped her cheek, his heated gaze searched hers. "Everything is fine. Now I want what I've craved for a long time."

His mouth covered her trembling lips. His tongue swept into her mouth sending heat to flood her mind and body. Strong hands pressed on her shoulders, until her back touched the fur of the rug and his hard body covered hers. Each thrust of his tongue into her mouth ratcheted up her need for more. His body felt tight beneath her fingers as if he struggled to control his movements.

"I can't wait any longer. You drive me insane." He wiped his mouth with the back of his hand as if he couldn't decide to drink her in one long draw or to savor her in small sips. "You are perfection," he said in a voice filled with raw emotion.

His fingers stroked her hair and then caressed her neck,

his lips following the path. His cock built a friction against her clit, moving back and forth. He lifted his head and looked into her eyes. Her mouth reached toward his for another kiss. He grabbed her hair, stopping her.

He asked, "Do you want this? Do you want me?" His dark eyes gazed into hers.

"Yes." She sounded like a snake as the word was drawn out. Her fingers dug into his scalp, trying to bring his lips to hers.

He pulled her arms up, holding them above her head with one hand as his other gripped her hair.

"Do you trust me to take care of you? I promise, before this night ends, you will climax so many times, you'll never want another man."

"I've never had anyone promise that." She couldn't resist teasing him by licking her lips. He groaned. Using the fistful of hair, he shook her head. It didn't hurt. If anything she found it intoxicating as he controlled her.

"Answer my question." His eyes narrowed to fierce slits.

"Yes. You'd never hurt me, unless I asked you to." A little bit of her wild youth showed through that answer.

His head jerked back, releasing her wrists. The smile she loved flashed in the firelight. She liked surprising him. Did he ever laugh out loud? He was so solemn. Well, except for his few smiles. Using the tip of a finger, she brushed the lines fanning near the outer corner of his eye. He laughed often, she thought.

"You're right," he whispered in her ear.

Then he plunged into her. She gasped from the pleasure of being filled, stretched close to her limit. He'd released his control, and she held on as he hammered into her. She needed it as much as he did.

Each thrust brought exquisite pleasure. Filling, retreating, filling her until his groin met hers. Their stamina matched, flesh slapped flesh until finally she climaxed. He let go, pumping to a slow stop to ensure their orgasms lasted longer.

John fell back, taking her with him. She nestled against his neck, a hand on his chest as he took care of the condom before he tightened his hold on her. His heated musk intoxicated her. His heartbeat raced as hard as hers. Unable to stop the need to explore, her hand drifted down his torso. She traced a vein down his cock, causing it to jerk from her attention as it lengthened and hardened again. She cupped his tight balls and squeezed. His hips lifted as he moaned. That fast, he was ready for more. She licked his neck.

A strong inhale escaped his lips and brought a pleased smile to her face. She no longer worried if she was doing it right.

Chapter Four

Lena began to move down his body when he captured her hands and rolled over, elbows locked, with only his groin to hers. "Wait. I'll be back in a moment."

Frustrated that he stopped her, she pouted and huffed, feeling like a sex kitten for the first time in her life. A pleased look crossed his face, and he said, "I like that your passion matches mine." He traced her lower lip with his finger. "We have plenty of time to explore. The night is still hours from ending."

She melted with each word.

"I'm glad. There's so much more I want to know about you...and your body." She smiled, and he kissed her cheek before he stood.

Her gaze followed as he strode barefoot and deliciously naked behind a *fusuma*. She heard water running and a few moments later he returned with a warm damp cloth and towel.

He pushed her hands away when she reached for them.

"No. Let me take care of you." Using the cloth, he ran it

up between her legs and parted her folds. She moaned, enjoying his soothing touch, as the ultra-soft material rubbed over the swollen area. He took an inordinate amount of time tracing every crease and dip. She'd never been treated so tenderly or examined so closely. His heated look eliminated any awkwardness.

"I was rough on you. Are you sensitive? Sore?" His concern reassured her.

"No. I'm fine. It was perfect." She looked down, embarrassed to say it but wanting him to understand. "I love how rough you are with me."

"Good." He tossed the cloth onto the tile in front of the fireplace. "Now let me show you how gentle I can be."

His fingers wrapped around her ankles, and he pushed her knees toward her ears. Before she could catch her breath his mouth covered her, and he licked from anus to clit before concentrating on her swollen flesh. Her back arched with each swipe of his tongue. He nipped at the tender nub and thrust into her delicate passage. A finger joined his tongue. Then a second one as his mouth moved to suck on the knot of nerves.

She opened her mouth, trying to draw in enough air. Finally, she shouted, "John!" and her body tightened and released with each wave.

Without hesitation, his arms slipped behind her knees and back and he lifted her as he stood.

Her fingers clutched his hair and brought his head down. She bit his ear.

He groaned and said in a husky voice, "I love it when you're rough."

She laughed as he carried her down a wide hallway. The twinkle in his eyes said he enjoyed teasing her.

"I want you to hurry to wherever you're carrying me. It

better be your bed." She caressed his neck and chest. "Even with a rug, that floor isn't...well, let's say I prefer a bed."

"Such a wimp. Maybe I sleep on a *shikibuton*." He looked into her face and burst out laughing. She suspected the *shikibuton* was a thin mattress on the floor. Astounded by his amusement at her expense, she grinned back. Why had she thought he never laughed? Her grin widened. Then again, what man wouldn't be in a better mood or have a great sense of humor after what they'd done and what they planned to do?

Lena found the house to be even more fascinating the deeper John carried her into it, a mixture of Western and Japanese furniture and design. Then they came to two large panels decorated with mountains, trees, and samurais riding beautiful fat horses. One samurai caught her attention. He had neon blue hair. She blinked. Then the scene disappeared. He'd slid open a panel.

The bedroom looked to be half a football field in size. On one end, a sunken hot tub quietly bubbled with water lilies drifting along the surface. It looked to be merely a dip in the floor as the tub's wood was slightly darker than the rest. Two white fluffy towels waited for them at one corner. The other end of the room held a massive pedestal bed with the thickest mattress she'd ever seen. There were two black lacquer chests of drawers facing opposite walls beside the bed. In the dim light, she couldn't make out the numerous photos scattered on the walls. They were the only ones she'd seen in the house so far.

Her attention shifted back to John when her toes met warm water, and he slowly released her.

"Oh, that feels good." Floating for a moment, she started to move away, but he pulled her into his lap as he sat in the water.

"No. I want to hold you." He wrapped his arms around her waist. Then his hands came up and cupped her breasts. She leaned her head back and kissed his chin. The man was an artist with his hands. She wondered if it had anything to do with his martial arts skills. Such magical touches, firm one moment and soft the next. His fingers massaged and pinched and tugged her nipples.

She moaned.

He lifted her torso and sucked in a taut nipple. Her nails dug into his shoulders, holding on as so many sensations overwhelmed her. Two thick fingers thrust between her legs as his mouth drew harder, taking turns at each breast.

Those talented fingers continued their rhythm as he licked and nibbled. Her hips moving, wanting more, wanting it harder. In seconds, she cried out his name again.

"Please, John. You're killing me." She loved how he took his time and played with her body as if he received as much pleasure as he gave. Tingles raced across her body.

"I would never do that," he said in a gruff voice. His eyes glittered.

Somewhere in the back of her mind a shiver raced down her spine. The rumor and his unspoken confirmation said he could be the man to do that.

Again, he lifted her and sat her on the edge of the hot tub. This time he pampered her by drying her body and the tips of her hair that had fallen into the water. With her in his arms, he strode over to the bed.

"You know I can walk."

"Are you sure?" He raised one eyebrow and let her body slide lusciously down his own.

On second thought, she tested her toes and then her knees. Her legs felt like limp noodles. Looking into his face, she teased, "Who am I to keep a strong man from showing off?"

"Humph!" He grinned and then pushed her back onto the mattress, and she sank into softness, reaching out for him. A heartbeat later he gathered her into his arms.

Boneless, she relaxed against his chest. Never had she experienced so many climaxes in one night or been more satisfied by a man than she had with John.

<<<>>>

Every move Lena made hardened John's cock even more.

He'd never responded so quickly to a woman's touch. For that matter, it took only a look. With her whiskey eyes and sable hair, and soft creamy pale skin beneath his callused fingers, after the destructive life he'd led she invoked feelings he'd only imagined were possible.

She pressed her lips to his neck and then collarbone. Her hair brushed his chest and stomach as wet warmth enclosed the tip of his cock. His body bowed as she sucked him, not stopping until her breath tickled the hair at his groin. Yes! A modest woman with erotic abilities he never expected.

He gasped as her tongue pressed underneath and followed the veins back up to the tip. Whatever she'd done at the head had his cock stretching tighter. Then she inhaled his hardness to the root again. With a quick move, he pulled away and cried out, releasing his appreciation on his stomach. Had he ever climaxed so fast from a blow job?

Hot whiskey eyes stared up at him. Years of working for a clandestine company had taught him to take life as it came and that included the good moments. Lena rated as the finest.

Clasping her upper arms, he brought her to eye level.

"Stay the weekend." His words sounded more like a command than a question, but he wanted her to understand.

She stared at him for a moment. His gut tightened as he expected her to say no. Despite the fact that they had had sex already, they were still strangers.

"Of course." She lightly pressed her lips to his. "I had a feeling I wouldn't be leaving until we had enough of each other."

Teeth clenched tight, he wanted to say, "That would never happen," but he knew it would end soon, no matter what he wanted. He pulled her close and kissed her forehead before pressing her cheek over his heart.

"Rest. There will be more." Before he finished the sentence her soft breath brushed his chest.

<<<>>>

In the middle of the night, Lena woke to being tossed face down on the bed. John shoved her knees toward her stomach, raising her ass, and then he brought her to the edge of the bed.

"This is an interesting way to say you want me," she teased.

"There are so many ways to appreciate your loveliness." He nearly grunted each word. His fingers slid into her. "You've recovered too. Wet and hot."

Without another word, he plunged into her. The sting of his hard entry was quickly replaced with pleasurable fullness. Each slide in and out built a need for more until she felt ripples start her release. His hand moved to her clit and he pinched. She screamed as the orgasm shook her body. She went limp, and he twisted a nipple, shooting sparks down her chest straight to her clit.

"What was that for?" She glared over her shoulder.

He grabbed her hair and pulled, bringing her ear nearer. He said in that husky whisper she loved, "Again." He bit her lobe, making her roar. "I want you to come for me again, and you know you love it." His thrusts increased in speed and depth.

Damn it, he was right. Never would she have believed she craved simultaneous pain and pleasure until he served it up to her. How was it that everything he did generated a deeper desire?

One hand still held her hair while the other grasped a hip—bruises would show later for sure—controlling her movements, taking her to a new height. Each lunge of his hips carried her body skyward. His hand moved from her hip to where her buttocks separated. He rotated his slick thumb over the smaller opening, pushing a little more on each pass until he'd entered to the knuckle.

The move surprised her, but the strange feeling was more than titillating. She shouted his name as he roared hers.

Chapter Five

The sound of bubbling water woke Lena. Lifting her head, she looked for John but was unsurprised to find herself alone. She laughed on realizing her head was inches from the foot of the bed. At least, what she considered to be the foot as the other end was next to a wall. It had been a crazy night. She also spotted, between the bed and the hot tub, a low table overflowing with food: bowls of fresh fruit and different flavors of dips, steaming bacon and two huge omelets.

She sat up and groaned. Her whole body ached, even her toes. Then she remembered John pumping into her from behind and her digging her toes into the mattress as she met his thrusts. Her face reddened when she recalled how wild she'd been.

But just before daylight, he'd made the sweetest love to her, holding and caressing as if he wanted to memorize every inch. They fell asleep in each other's arms, so contented.

Where was he?

As she expected John to show up any minute and determined to enjoy her time with him, she wrapped the comforter around her—unable to locate a sheet—and stumbled her way over to the bathroom panel. A few minutes later, she returned, still no John, and fell on one of the cushions next to the table. Next to her plate was a small note. John had written that she should eat all she wanted as he had a call to the east to handle before daybreak. And that he would return soon.

The food tasted divine. She was unsure if it was from the talents of the cook or her wonderfully strenuous night.

After eating half of the food, she decided to look for something to wear, maybe a shirt of his. No way would she go wandering through his house naked, searching for her clothes and John. She dropped the comforter. Before she reached the nearest chest, her attention was drawn by the group of pictures above it.

A naked woman tied with rope to an outside light pole similar to the ones that had lined John's drive was in the first picture. As she studied each picture with a different woman tied on different out- and indoor structures, she had to admit the knot patterns, the positions of the women and their various surroundings had an exotic beauty. Maybe he was only fascinated with the art.

So many pictures. From what she'd seen of John, he wasn't the type to hang random snapshots in his most private space, especially erotic in nature. He'd taken them. She was certain.

Frowning, she looked again at each picture. The women appeared to be in a daze. She didn't like the thought of John touching and tying up strange women. Had no one ever held his interest for long? A flush covered her face and neck.

She wanted to be the one. She wanted his attention centered on her and no one else.

She crossed her arms as her nipples tightened. The thought of John tying her up, stretching the rope in and around sensitive areas, and taking complete control brought a strange sensation racing through her body.

Pulling her gaze from the pictures—she needed clothes—she opened a drawer, hoping to find a towel or shirt. Instead she found red rope. In the next drawer she found blue and in the next green. She picked up a coil. How strange, it wasn't rough, but smooth.

"Lena?"

She turned to John. Dressed in loose fitting black pants hanging off his hips, no shirt, and with his shaggy hair hiding one eye, he was gorgeous and wild. A small flash of concern darted over his face.

"These aren't just art pictures. You took them," she stated. She used the rope to point at the nearest frame.

"Yes. I'm a *nawashi*, rope master, of *kinbaku*." His dark eyes watched her behind the cold mask that he now wore as if to protect himself.

Confused by it all, she looked away for a second. What did he expect her to say? Being truthful to herself, she wasn't sure what she should feel.

"So you're into S and M?" A chill brushed her skin, reminding her she stood before him naked. While still holding the rope, she dangled it below her waist while she crossed her other hand to the opposite breast, covering as much as possible. She felt so stupid. He'd seen every square inch of her. There really wasn't a need to hide, but she couldn't drop her hands.

"*Kinbaku* is the sensual art of bondage." With unhurried and studied movements as if he believed she would bolt, he lifted the green rope out of her hands. "The *jujun*, one who submits to the rope, will find the rope and the placements of the knots to be an experience not easily forgotten." He slowly wrapped one folded end around her wrists and knotted it before pulling her closer until her breasts pressed into his bare skin. "The combination of the patterns and the beautiful positioning of the female body are erotically stimulating to the *nawashi* and *jujun*. Many find the feeling to be releasing, and they often learn to crave the touch."

As if in a trance, she concentrated on every word and touch. His voice soothed her doubts and his touch brought a desire for more.

"Sweet one, I can show you that side of your sensuality, the side that wants me to take control. You know I would never hurt you or do anything that wouldn't bring you pleasure."

Subconsciously, she was aware he was walking her backwards to the bed. His hands grasped her waist, and he pushed her backward onto the mattress.

Her mind whirled from the erotic images invoked by his words. They turned her on but was she giving him too much of herself? Though heat infused her with need, deep inside she trembled with the unknown.

"I'm nervous," she admitted.

"I'll go slow." He smoothed her hair from her forehead. Eyes cool and distant earlier now looked at her with hot desire. "All you have to say is stop," he said in a low gentle voice. "Simple, right?"

She nodded.

As he raised her hands above her head, his hardness pressed into her folds. His mouth dipped down and nipped at a tender breast. She gasped.

She was so turned on she even heard a buzzing sound.

Wait. It wasn't her. It was real. A buzzing came from around her. What was happening? A fire?

"Fuck!" He quickly untied her hands. "Get dressed." He pressed a button behind one of the pictures and a door opened. "Your clothes are in here. We need to leave in five minutes. Don't make me throw you into the car naked."

"What's going on?" She reached her feet and swayed. Her body hadn't caught on that it needed to walk. Disoriented, she blinked and looked around.

He stopped what he was doing and grabbed her shoulders to stare into her eyes.

"Unwelcome visitors are on the property. You're safe, if you follow my instructions." Then he kissed her hard and quick before he released her. With a tender caress of her cheek, he said, "Hurry."

He reached into the darkness and then pitched her clothes toward her. Seconds later, he pulled on a shirt and a shoulder holster with gun. He disappeared into the hidden room, and she heard him talking to someone.

"How many? Okay." With a cell phone to his ear, he returned and a frown wrinkled his forehead. He tugged on a black leather jacket while still listening to whoever was on the other end. "Hold them off, we're leaving."

The next hour was surreal. He hustled her into his car and barely cleared the opening garage door as he sped down his driveway. When she looked out the back windshield, she caught silhouettes moving around the exterior of the house. Their rifles swinging toward the drive were identifiable against the bright backdrop. The appearance of the whole building had changed. All of the panels were closed facing the windows. John had mentioned earlier that besides the bulletproof glass, there were other security measures. She had a feeling not all of the panels were rice paper.

Then the car's back glass shattered into a spider-web pattern, but no hole appeared, and what sounded like rocks dinged against the sedan.

She wanted to scream and cry and have a breakdown, but kept thinking how John depended on her to keep it together. Her heart thudded against her chest in pure terror, but everything felt unreal. Every movement slowed into another universe or time warp or whatever scientists called this moment of full blown adrenaline.

He pressed her head down.

Unable to handle not knowing, keeping her nose pressed to the plastic trim of the door, she peeked out and saw that one side of the gate twisted on the ground several feet from the entry. Someone had rammed the weakest part of the fortification. Dark lumps spotted the grassy areas. Her stomach churned when she realized they were bodies.

He pushed her back down.

Who were these people trying to kill him? Why couldn't she shout and let them know she wasn't the one they wanted? Common sense told her they wouldn't care. The darkness equalized friend and foe.

"Stay there," he demanded.

Who was she to argue? Too scared to move more than a couple inches, she obeyed. She'd never been in this type of situation. His calm attitude confirmed this wasn't his first rodeo.

A few minutes later, he told her it was safe to sit up. Staring out the window, she looked for landmarks in the dark. Where were they? The car sped down the road, the trees a blur in the predawn light. Never in her life had she experienced such...chaos. Danger.

She opened her mouth a couple times before sound came out. "Those weren't rocks hitting the side of the car or the back windshield, were they?" Her whole body shook. She rubbed the chill bumps on her arms. She'd known what they were but wanted him to say it.

"No. The car is bulletproof." In the dim light from the dashboard, the anger on his face frightened her. If he ever caught the people, she felt certain their deaths wouldn't be easy. "I should've never brought you to my home. I knew it was dangerous but my sources told me that they were days away." He banged his fist on the steering wheel. "I'm sorry I endangered you out of my own selfishness."

"I'm safe. That's all that matters," she said. Scared spitless but safe, she thought. The trembling started to ease off.

"Yes. You're right." He glanced her way, his expression softened. "Once I get you away from them, you'll be perfectly safe. Each time I drove to your house, I took detours, backtracked. I even had decoys working to draw away anyone who would follow me. We used every trick. They never followed me to your house."

That explained why he always rushed her to his car. Why she felt like he drove in circles on the way to his house the evening before. Besides, the black sedan never fit into the type of car she expected he'd own. The ones she'd seen in the garage were more his type.

After many turns, and what was certainly backtracking, they arrived at her front door.

"I'll have one of my men watch your house for a few days." He stepped out of the car and opened the passenger door for her. "Be observant and don't let anyone inside."

When his hand held her arm, she realized small tremors shook every inch of her body.

She asked, "Will you be okay?"

Seeing him again felt important. He'd taught her so much, and she wanted to be with him a little longer and see if it all had been real. No one had ever made her feel so much like a sexual, desirable woman. She'd lost count of how many times he'd given her an orgasm. Whoever thought that happened in real life?

"I enjoyed our time together," he said in a flat tone.

The cold look on his face brought a flush to her face. She would be a one-night stand after all? That was it? They'd walked about halfway to the front door when a blur whizzed by, knocking her down.

John's hands and feet shot out, knocking the person to the ground several yards away. Then out of the dark, several more men dressed in black swarmed over John. Barely a shriek left her mouth when a hand jerked her to her feet and another covered her mouth. The person pulled her toward a dark SUV.

The sound of kicks and hits landing on solid flesh sickened Lena. They were beating him to death. She struggled against her captor, and before he could throw her into the open door, the mound of people exploded. Several of the dark figures stayed motionless on the ground.

John ran toward her, leaping over one attacker, appearing to fly through the air. His foot slammed into the face of the man holding her. Astoundingly, when John hit the ground, he retained his balance. Was he human?

"Come." He clasped her wrist and pushed her into the SUV and then jumped into the other side. With the motor running, he simply shoved the gear into drive. Tires squealed as they shot down her street, heading toward Interstate Five.

All of it continued to feel surreal. Her insides shook as she glanced at her reflection in the dark window. Who was that shell-shocked person?

Who was this man she'd fallen in love with? Oh, my

God! How could she be in love with someone she'd only begun to know? Just because they had good sex—no, scratch that—mind-blowing sex, didn't mean they were going to marry or...she was as crazy as he was and the night was beyond insane.

Chapter Six

Hell, what was he going to do with her?

John pressed the gas a little harder, taking the curve nearly on two wheels. He glanced over to her sweet worried face. His hands tightened on the steering wheel. Every precaution he'd taken with her had been for shit. She should've been secured.

His informant sucked and would soon be a dead man. John had been told Inferno was another week out from attacking. He wasn't sure if he was more pissed for his weekend plans being royally screwed or for nearly getting them killed. His intention to satiate his every need for Lena before completing his final Circle assignment had disintegrated with the gunfire.

Sure, taking out a chunk of Inferno's force guaranteed he would be left alone long enough for others to take over the mission of their annihilation. He planned to live in retirement without looking over his shoulder. He sneered. Well, as much as he could with others wanting his balls on a rack. But the assholes had closed in faster than expected.

He checked the rearview mirror. Loosening his grip to

better handle the car, he turned hard at the next right. His arm slung out to hold Lena in an effort to keep her from slamming into the dashboard or the passenger door.

Another check on her. He was happy to see that, though pale, she handled all the excitement rather well. And he had a feeling more danger was to come.

There was always the possibility another group had found him. He'd done everything but throw out breadcrumbs for Inferno to locate him. How easy would it be for another group to pick up on the trail? Damn! His mind raced with so many possibilities. The Yakuza? The numerous bad guys he'd helped take down for The Circle? He knew better than to leave behind so many living and breathing enemies. But it hadn't always been left to his discretion. The higher-ups often changed their minds about the elimination of the enemy, especially if they had a special skill that could be put to good use.

"I believe I deserve to know who's after you since they're keeping me away from my home." She stabbed a finger at him. "They almost kidnapped me," she said with a tremor in her voice. "Why would they want me?"

Damn, he hated that she was afraid. Yet she'd handled so much of it better than most civilians would.

As he'd admitted to her earlier, because of his own self-ishness. What was wrong with wishing for a little normalcy? He had to go and involve Lena in his crazy world. How often had someone he cared about been touched by the evil that shadowed him? His half-sister found that out the hard way when she'd been kidnapped by sex slavers. No matter that he'd rescued her before she'd been harmed, she'd rushed back home to Japan never wanting to see him again.

A heavy, tight feeling clenched his throat with the thought. His sister had been the only light to his short stay in Japan, and he'd been thrilled when she looked him up in the States. That didn't last long. He'd wished many times that he'd sent her back on a plane as soon as she'd shown up, saving her from that horrific experience.

"John?" Lena's eyes begged for an explanation.

"They've been coming after me for the last few years. It's a group called Inferno. The bastards want me dead. They had hoped to purchase some high-tech bullets, but I provided information to the organization I worked for that put a crimp in the manufacture and shipment of what was called Hell's Purifier. So killing me would be their method of punishment." Actually, they wanted to wound him, haul his barely breathing body to an undisclosed place and beat the hell out of him until he died. At least, that was what the head of the organization he worked for told him, with obvious glee, after John said he was retiring — quitting really as they didn't expect anyone to live long enough to do otherwise — after this assignment. "I've interfered a couple times with their ultimate goal of destroying civilization. So they can rebuild it under their ideology." The car rattled and shook as he turned onto a dirt road.

"You're kidding. Right? Why would anyone want to do that? That's crazy."

He could tell her, but that would include explaining the type of life he led. Hers had been a normal one until she met him. The less she knew the better off she'd be at this point.

"You're staying with me for a little longer. Until I stop them or they lose interest in you." He refused to think of the third option. Her death.

"How could harming me help them?"

When the car entered a large clearing, he pressed the brake and turned off the headlights. Facing her, he said,

"They're counting on me giving myself up to protect you." He cupped her chin. "I'd never allow that."

"Oh." The lone light from a nearby building lit up her face, showing her eyes wide in surprise as she clasped his hand. "Thank you."

"I like that."

"I don't understand." Her forehead wrinkled.

"You understood what I was trying to say. You knew that I would come after you, no matter what. And you're not afraid of me."

"Deep inside, I feel I can trust you. If I had felt differently, I'd have never stepped into the sedan with you, and certainly wouldn't have had sex with you."

How many years had it been since a woman smiled at him like that? Filled with desire and the conviction he would protect her with his life.

"Good. Time for you to trust me further." He held out his hand.

Without hesitation, she placed hers in his, and he soaked in her gorgeous smile. He tugged her closer and kissed her. Her lips trembled beneath his. Everything about this woman excited him. How would he ever let her go?

<<<>>>

If someone had told Lena last week that she would be flying in a private plane to an unknown destination, she'd be asking what lottery had she won? Granted the plane was no more than a two-seater with a large cargo area in the back—she really didn't want to think what he normally hauled—but he'd warned her they'd be flying to Denver at the usual altitudes. Once they refueled, they'd fly low, stopping a couple more times before they reached the end of the trip. All he'd said about that was she would enjoy white sand beneath the moon. So she knew they wouldn't come to the end of their trip until evening and it would be at a beach.

She did know whatever happened next, she wanted to be with him. When he decided it was safe for her to go home, she would go without begging, if that was what he insisted on. She had a little pride.

After landing in Kansas City to refuel, they headed southeast, flying low to stay below radar. Hours later, with her napping on and off, and taking a minute to call a couple friends and lying to them about her unexpected trip to Hawaii, he landed on a sandy strip in the middle of nowhere, near a large expanse of water off to one side. She gazed longingly between the trees at the water glinting in the moonlight.

"Where are we?" she asked.

John had finished helping another man push the plane into a large barn, and he sauntered back to her, wiping at the sweat running down the side of his face. The man did look good all glistening, hair tangled around his face.

"A few miles from Gulf Shores and Orange Beach. I have a house no one can trace us to."

"Lots of glass?" She grinned. Even in the short time she'd been around him, she sensed he hated enclosed places. Though open areas of sun and glass weren't healthy for him due to his dangerous work, whatever that was, he loved being able to see around him.

"Only facing the Gulf." He returned her smile and then clasped the back of her neck, holding her still as he covered her mouth with his. His tongue slid along hers and brought heat to the pit of her stomach and further down.

When his lips trailed down to her neck, she asked, "Where's your house?"

He chuckled.

She wanted to hear that sound forever.

"Come with me. We'll see if we can finish what we started." John brushed his lips against hers. Holding her hand, he pulled her to the other side of the barn where a parked white SUV waited for them.

His grip on her hand didn't ease as he drove up to a beautiful beach house sitting on stilts. No fences or men with rifles. She loved it, but what if they were attacked again?

"Are you sure we'll be safe?"

"It would take their techs at least thirty days with all the holding companies I used to purchase this place, and I'm giving them a benefit of some intelligence. It took them forty-five days to find my other house, and I wasn't trying to hide it so much."

"What do you mean?" She struggled to hide her horror at the thought of his carelessness in protecting himself.

"Enough of that. We have this moment. Tomorrow..." He tapped her chin with a finger. "We'll talk about the future tomorrow." He picked her up. His muscles shifted against her body as she wrapped trembling arms around his neck.

When he carried her through the front door, kicking off his shoes before stopping in the middle of the great room, she released a long exhale.

"You have great taste in views." The dark waves and long white beach sparkled in the light of the nearly full moon. The scene was framed by large panes of glass and centered in open French doors.

"Yes. I do."

She looked up and hunger appeared in his exotic eyes. Unable to hold back any longer, she threaded her fingers through his hair and lifted her face to meet his lips. Desire and liquid heat flowed over her. She wanted this man again.

Even deliciously sore, she craved more of what John could do.

Shoving open a door off the living room, he hesitated in the master bedroom. An enormous four-poster bed swathed with thin white material stood in the center. The breeze off the gulf moved the material, giving the room a dreamy quality.

He leaned over and spread her out in the center of the bed, covering her body with his.

"Remember what you discovered at my home before we were interrupted?"

She didn't need to ask what he meant. The intensity of that moment when she discovered his special hobby hadn't been far out of her thoughts during the trip. Each time he touched her arm to point out a beautiful mountain or pressed his hand to the small of her back as they stopped to refuel and stretch their legs, she wondered if the rope would feel as sensuous. Just knowing it would be John doing the tying and binding, she felt certain every sensation would be amplified.

"Yes." She grinned.

"I want to show you how desirable it can be. It'll change your life. Make you realize what you've been missing. Do you believe me?"

Her gaze dropped to his lips. They were thin, almost cruel looking, but he hadn't hurt her. He'd protected her.

She believed him when he'd said he worked hard at not bringing his past to her door. But the past was what fashioned them into who they were at that moment. How could she fault him? She certainly loved the person he was now.

"Yes. Show me," she whispered, desire deepening her voice until only a husky murmur escaped.

He kissed her, sweeping his tongue over hers as she teased his with a few tentative strokes. Why did she feel so shy at this point? *Silly girl, you have just given a man permission to tie you down.* The zing traveling from her heart to her groin alerted her to how much she wanted this.

He squeezed her tight, although he was careful. She'd seen what he did to those other men without using a gun. Deep inside she knew he'd never willingly harm her. She trusted him completely.

He moved away, trailing his hand down her body. "Take off your clothes. All of them."

The bed shifted as he stood and stripped off his shirt. He stepped over to a seven-foot-tall chifforobe and opened the mirrored door. Hanging from hooks were black, green, blue and red ropes.

She wrinkled her forehead when she spotted a large purple bruise across one rib and others sprinkled around his torso. Before she expressed her concerns, his graceful movements reassured her all was okay. The man amazed her. Was she strange to believe it enhanced his masculinity?

When he glanced her way, he said, "Lena. Now."

She shivered at the command, not in fear but in anticipation. Yes. She could've protested his stern tone, but she'd never been a hypocrite just on principle. She liked his bossiness. There was no danger in sight at the moment, and the obvious display of his cock pressed sideways against the front of his slacks easily gave away his true mood.

As she undressed, each movement was slow and sensual. Her husband had never watched her take her clothes off, but John hesitated in his handling of the rope to stare. His fascination caused her to draw out each reveal: a left breast and then right, the gradual slide of her jeans and panties down her legs. She'd never felt so alive and voluptuous.

"Come. Kneel here." He laid out a folded blanket on the floor.

She smoothly dropped to her knees in the soft center and then looked up at him as her butt rested on her heels.

His possessive look brought a flush to her whole body. His warrior stance brought pride to her chest as it dawned on her that the remarkable man before her wanted her in every way possible and as much as she did him.

"Hands behind your back." His fingers drifted down her arms as she complied without hesitation. "Your skin is like silk." He wrapped the black rope around her wrists.

"I thought the rope would feel rough." She wiggled her fingers.

"Be still," he gently admonished her. He moved to the side to look into her face. "There are different kinds of rope used in different kinds of play. I prefer to bring out your carnal beauty using the linen rope. No worry, sweet one. If you're in pain, there's no way I can achieve that. So relax and let me know if anything I do discomforts you."

When he didn't move she knew he was waiting for an answer. "Okay." She nodded and smiled.

His lips brushed hers before returning to his rope. "Be sure to stay still."

As he wrapped and threaded the rope above, below and between her breasts, he whispered encouragement.

"Look how your skin appears to glow. White and

smooth, made perfect for this. Such warmth beneath such paleness."

Her worries floated away. The sureness of his movements and the snugness of the rope brought a sense of being hugged, cared for. The pattern he created across her torso pushed out her breasts, making them appear fuller and aroused. Her nipples ached for his touch. Truthfully, each time his fingers brushed against her skin and pulled on the rope, she became more aware of every nerve ending. She wanted him to do more. To kiss her. To take her.

"Sweet one, lift up to your knees and part them."

She straightened her back and did as he asked. He helped as her wrists were not only wrapped together but her arms were bound too. His hand smoothed down her back and over a buttock before dipping between her legs to caress her labia. She sighed. His long fingers parted and slid through the wetness. She shivered with pleasure.

"Yes. This is making you wet. Good. You want this as much as I do." Then he pulled the rope between her legs, adjusted two lengths on each side and rested it in the crease of her thighs, framing the part that wanted more of his attention. "That's it. The rope enhances your beautiful creamy skin."

Unable to help it, she squirmed.

He pinched a buttock and just as quickly caressed the spot. "Be still. It won't be much longer, and I'll reward you for your cooperation and patience."

The tinge of pain mixed with pleasure kicked up her desire several hundred notches. Bondage and pain? She had no idea she was that type of woman. Then again, her unusual reaction stemmed from the man administering it.

As he continued to wrap her in the rope, he'd stop every couple minutes and slip his hand behind the rope and tug on it. She quickly realized he was testing it, making sure of its fit. He didn't want it too tight. He'd promised no pain. Well, none from the rope.

She relaxed once against as he worked down each leg. The rhythm of tucking and tugging rocked her until every muscle eased its tension. She felt like she floated above the floor.

"Sweet one, here, lean back. Let me help." He held her shoulders as he placed her on her back. While she'd been in her little trance, he'd moved a few pillows behind her. The softness protected her wrists, keeping her from cutting off her circulation. "Now pull your heels to your buttocks."

"John, I'm not sure." Though still turned on, she didn't like the thought of being so open.

"Shh, I'm the only one here. If you become scared, just tell me. I promise I'll stop, but I know you'll find it gratifying."

His reassuring tone calmed her more than the words. Besides, with his hands smoothing and massaging her skin, including the parts covered with rope, her breathing quickened. She lifted her legs and his hands grabbed her ankles. Rope circled one ankle and he pulled it back looping part of it through the rope at her thighs. Then he did the same with the other ankle.

She looked across her torso. With one knee on the floor, barefooted and bare-chested, wearing only his black pants, John leaned forward with a sense of awe on his face and cupped her mons.

"Your flesh is pink, blossoming with desire." He murmured a few more words she didn't understand.

"John, please." She arched into his touch as he pressed two fingers into her. Her eyes drifted closed as he thrust in rhythm with her heartbeat. Then his hand moved away.

She whimpered with need.

A zipper clicked its way down. Flesh, warm and hard, slid into her. She welcomed the feeling of fullness. Then heat covered her.

"You're so tight, so wet for me. Your body is ready for whatever pleasure I give you."

She opened her eyes.

John leaned over her with his arms straight near her shoulders as his hips moved. He began slowly, pumping at a leisurely pace. Her breath caught. Wrapped and knotted in rope, she could only yield. She delighted in the freedom of not worrying where to place her hands or moving the right way. He did all the work, and she received so much pleasure. The rope securely held her for whatever pleased him, and in turn, pleased her. With each thrust the rope moved, not scraping but tightening, releasing in the same beat. Her nipples engorged to the point that whenever his chest brushed hers, she moaned from the stimulation.

"Please. Please harder."

He looked down into her eyes and smiled. The warmth in his gaze said he understood what she felt, and there was more. He picked up speed, pounding into her wetness. He shifted, cupped her ass and lifted her to his lap. She felt as if he held every inch of her securely in his arms.

She screamed, and a moment later, his shout equaled hers.

For a woman who never begged for sex or raised her voice during the act, she continued to find herself rather vocal with the man holding her so gently in his arms.

Chapter Seven

John pulled out of her and sat back on his heels. From sweet toes to lovely face, her tender skin glowed different shades of pink. He loosened the rope at her thighs and began to unknot each section, kissing the impressions left behind.

"Did I hurt you?" He'd never forgive himself if she was harmed. His experience said he'd been careful, but he wanted her assurance all was well. No regrets.

"I don't believe so. Unless I pulled something when I had the biggest orgasm in my life." She laughed.

Every minute with Lena showed what a miracle it was that he'd met her. She proved to be everything he'd ever wanted from a woman: brave, sexy, modest in words but an adventurer in bed.

"You're a fearless woman. Your beautiful soul overwhelms me."

"I love how you talk. It's like poetry." A lopsided grin brightened her sweet face. "When can we do this again?"

He chuckled. "I promise that we will do it often. But first I must untie you." He pressed his lips against one marked thigh. The red patterns brought a rush of blood and heat to his cock again. Unable to resist, he covered her with his mouth and licked her hardened clit. He heard her sharp intake of breath. She widened her legs. Without hesitation he sucked until she lifted her hips to meet his mouth. He pressed his thumb into her wetness and then moved it further down, slipping it into a tighter orifice. The adorable sounds she emitted assured him she enjoyed his attention. "Soon I'll take you there, and you'll love it even more." He ran his tongue over her little knot and then pulled it with his teeth.

She gasped and her body tightened and released over and over again.

"I've never met a man like you. How do you know? How do know what I want without me telling you?" Her eyes sparkled with wonder.

He smiled as he continued to remove the ropes. When he finished, he massaged her shoulders as her arms had been tied the longest.

<<<>>>

Once her arms quit tingling, Lena turned and clasped his face between her hands. "John, what's next? I don't want to think of losing you now that we've found each other. Geez, that sounds so cliché." Her fingers threaded into the long cool strands of his hair. She'd never been crazy about long hair, even hair that only reached the collar, but she loved how his felt against her breasts and thighs as he kissed her all over. "Yet, you live a dangerous life. I have no skills to help you, but I want to be with you. Please don't leave me after this." She cringed at the pleading tone in her voice.

"Ah, my sweet one. I'd give my life to keep you from

harm and keep you by my side." He pulled her close and lightly brushed his lips over hers. "You must know that a man in love will walk through fire to protect his woman." His hands swept up her torso and cupped her breasts, squeezing them deliciously tight. "And I'm that man and you're that woman." His kiss deepened as if he wanted to brand her with his mouth.

<<<>>>

The next few weeks were heaven on earth to Lena. She spent most days naked and beneath John. He massaged lotions into her skin to guard her from the sun and oils to shield her from the rope he wrapped her in.

She shifted on the lounge chair beneath the umbrella and winced. He'd made good his promise from their first night at the beach house, and she found sitting to be a tender position.

"Are you all right, sweet one?" John grasped her hand and kissed the back, his dark eyes twinkling as he knew why she was having difficulties.

Maybe she should return the favor, but considering how he loved being in control—she sighed—and how much she loved his being in control, she doubted that would ever happen. Her gaze caressed his bare body. The sun had been kind to him. His skin was golden brown, unbroken by tan lines. No sign of bruises. She licked every inch, especially the part that was lengthening beneath her stare.

"Oh, I'm better than fine." Her skin had tanned slightly but with a soft pink glow. He'd told her it looked like the inside of one of the shells they'd found. Without a second thought, she moved off the chair and kneeled next to him and clasped his cock. When she looked up, his face was solemn, watching her intensely. Her eyes still on his, she licked the head of his cock, pressing her tongue in the small groove before she sucked him in hard.

"Arrgh." He threw back his head and pushed his hips at her mouth.

She drew him in further until her tongue almost touched his testicles. For the last week, she'd practiced, going deeper each time. Her hand lifted and rolled the sensitive sac. With each lick and suck, she felt his balls tighten. Then he grabbed her hair and pulled her away. His ejaculation sprayed his belly and chest.

Using a beach towel, she helped clean him off. She grinned with satisfaction. He came faster than he had when she'd gone down on him during breakfast. Surprising him was such a thrill.

He brought her closer and nipped at her bottom lip. "Thank you."

She giggled. When was the last time she'd giggled? She didn't care. John made her happier than she ever remembered. Her hand cupped his dear face.

"I love you." She finally said it. No way could she hold it in any longer.

Though he didn't say the same words, his eyes told her so much. They warmed and softened as if he was letting her inside, allowing her to see what no one else had before. His thumb caressed her lips. In her heart, she was certain he'd never been so relaxed and so giving to anyone as he had been to her. He'd changed from the stiff formal man from their first date to a more loving and open partner. For that matter she'd changed too. Always afraid of what others would think of her if they knew the wildness wanting out or how she would disappoint James if she expressed her true opinion. Hell, she even had a tattoo now. She peeked at the butterfly on top of her foot as she wiggled her toes.

John lifted her chin and whispered, "It's about time you told me." His teasing brought a big smile to her face. As if he couldn't resist, he leaned down to kiss her. His tongue danced with hers. She wanted more, always wanted more when he touched her.

An explosion broke the silence as the ground shook and debris sprinkled their umbrella.

"Oh, my God!" She landed on her back in the sand.

John jumped over her to ward off the men spilling down onto the beach from the flaming beach house. Being magnificently naked didn't slow him as he picked up a chair and swung it at a couple men, knocking them down. In a smooth move he picked up an evil-looking long gun from one of the fallen men.

Numb with fear, Lena wanted to help but knew she'd be in the way. How could she help when she'd never held a gun or hit another human being? If she lived, and once they escaped, the first order of business was to learn how to protect herself, and possibly help the man she loved.

When he sprayed the area with gunfire, she squeezed her eyes shut. Who was she kidding? They were outnumbered, and John was fierce but no man could protect himself and her. She bit her lip, trying to keep from crying out. The smell of blood and death mixed with the salt air. Her stomach turned over.

Throwing up will distract him, throwing up will distract him, she repeated silently.

The barrage persisted, echoing in the distance with the screams from the wounded. Though it felt like hours, she knew it had been mere minutes. Somehow John continued to fight, holding the men back. She cried, covering her head with her arms, certain they were doomed as she waited for the bullets to tear into her body. She hated feeling so helpless.

"Lena. Sweet one. Shh!" John's voice was calm.

Shouting surrounded her, but no more gunfire.

She opened one eye. John kneeled next to her. Sand and dark smears covered parts of his body. *Thank you, God, he's alive.* She ran her hands over his body, checking for wounds. She could at least patch him up. She'd taken a first-aid class years ago.

"I'm fine. Everything's okay." He looked her over too.

Her legs shook as he helped her stand. She looked around. Men in black uniforms surrounded some of the motley crew who had been attacking. Other black-clad men carried the wounded or dead off the beach.

"What happened?" She fell into his arms, holding him tight with her face pressed to his chest.

"Inferno attacked sooner than expected. Again. You're a gutsy woman." He tightened his hold on her while keeping a grip on the gun. "If they had waited one more evening, we would've been gone from here."

"I hid and cried. Some guts."

He pressed his lips to her neck and softly said, "Even though you were scared, you didn't do anything foolish."

Embarrassed by his praise, she asked, "Where did the men who saved us come from?" She leaned back to look into his eyes.

Another deep voice piped in, "I couldn't let my best agent get killed just before he retires."

John's eyes narrowed, "Yeah, right. I've done my part

and pulled them out. Now it's up to you to get the intel that you need. I'm retired as of this moment."

Lena turned and barely held in a gasp. Scars covered the side of the man's face. A patch hid one eye, but that didn't prevent him from glowering at her.

"Best agent?" Unsure if she heard correctly, she looked up at John.

"Lena, this is Ryker. He's the head of The Circle organization. My former employer as of...about thirty seconds ago."

"The Circle?" There was so much she didn't know about John.

"We provide security for those who can afford it, among other things," Ryker said. Then he turned to John and took his gun. "Ice, we'll clean up this mess. You have a nice trip." He nodded toward Lena, giving her a lopsided grin that she found rather frightening. Then he slapped John on the shoulder before walking off.

"John, were the people who attacked us the same ones from Seattle? And where are we going?"

Before he could answer another man dressed in black jogged over and handed John a stack of blankets. That was when Lena remembered they were naked. Thankfully, John had a tight hold on her, pressing her front to his side, or she would've died of humiliation. No wonder the man called Ryker looked at her so strangely. With her red face hidden in his shoulder, she clasped the edge of the blanket as he wrapped it around her.

"Yes. The same ones from Seattle. This should help deplete their numbers." John pressed a kiss to her nose. "We're going to a little island off the coast of Florida that Collin and Olivia sold me a few months ago. And I promise no one can trace me to it." He laughed. "At least, The Circle promised to place their resources behind protecting it and keeping it hidden." He caressed her cheek. "I had planned to move there next year, but I have a good reason to leave early."

"Me?" She tried to hold back the big grin but it broke free.

He smiled back and nodded. "Of course. And how about sailing to the island?" He pointed out to the gulf. Off in the distance was a boat with large blue and white sails.

"It's beautiful!"

"I've already confirmed the captain can marry us too." He caressed her face. His eyes looked at her so tenderly that she had no doubt he loved her. Over the last few weeks, he'd talked about being a man in love, but he never came straight out and said it. That wasn't his way. He preferred showing it instead.

"I love you too. And I'll be happy to marry you as long as you promise to show me more about *kinbaku*." She gave him a wicked grin.

"That's my sweet one." He rested an arm over her shoulder and began walking toward the water where a small motorboat was being shoved to shore. "And maybe tai chi."

"As long as you're the teacher. And you need to teach me how to shoot a gun and protect myself. I refused to stand around next time you're in danger."

"You appear determined. Okay. I do have a special hands-on technique." His teasing grin almost caused her knees to melt.

Her heart felt so light. "I've never been on a sailboat before."

"You'll like it."

"I hope I don't get seasick."

"No worry. The rocking motion will be our friend."

She frowned and then looked at him. The hungry look he gave her said it all. She blushed and said, "Maybe I need to start tying you up."

His laughter echoed over the water as they walked toward a brighter future.

Circle of Defiance

Chapter One

The sharp smell of blood and alcohol penetrated the cool air as the glass door closed behind Katerina Savalas. Hard rock blasted her ears. She hesitated and scanned the unfamiliar surroundings. Being in the less than safe side of town, she wanted to get her business done and over with as fast as possible.

Never in her wildest nightmares had she imagined stepping into such a place. When her dad kicked her out of the house, she'd sworn she'd find another way to express herself. Too many people believed it to be the perfect way to protest. Instead, it became a rebellion that led to a habit. Not for her. No way. Each to their own.

Looking at an intriguing drawing on the wall, she shook her head. Maybe it was a tiny bit tempting.

"Hello, pretty little girl, what can I do for you?" The man smiled and his skin pulled at the black swirling pattern covering one side of his face. A chain connected his pierced nose to a large spool in his ear and jingled when he moved around the counter. He stopped a little too close.

She swallowed, trying to keep her stomach from turning

upside down. Just thinking about a needle sinking into her skin gave her the willies. Taking another deep swallow to settle her long ago eaten cheeseburger, she forced her legs to stiffen and hold her up.

Wrenching her gaze away from the maltreated chunk of fat and skin, she looked over his shoulder to regain her composure.

"I was told Jack Drago's here," she nearly shouted to be heard over the music.

"Who told you that?" His tone was threatening.

"Phil at the Sandbox," she answered, straining to see around a curtain in the back of the room.

Whoever named the bar had thought they were cute, playing with Sand City's name. She agreed the place had been pretty decent as it sported a couple pool tables in the back and a small stage for local bands. Even on Tuesday nights, families gathered and enjoyed an old movie shown on a drop-down screen. A person could call the atmosphere homey, for a bar. She'd visited it several times since moving into the small town. But then again, the Sandbox being the only bar in town limited her choices.

The owner had told her to hang around until late that evening. Jack often showed up by nine. The problem with that was she didn't want to waste any more time. So he'd suggested checking into Lonnie's Place.

From what she'd seen so far of Lonnie's, she preferred the Sandbox Bar and Grill.

"Phil's going to get his ass beat, if he ain't careful. He knows better than to give out info about Jack."

"So he's here?" When the man's brow wrinkled in confusion, she added, "Jack. Is Jack here?"

The Mike Tyson wannabe leaned close, his onion-loaded breath bursting across her face. She moved back a step and pretended to scratch her nose. Anything to block the smell.

"Whatcha going to give me?" He grabbed her arm. "Everyone pays a toll." The leer told her what he expected.

Without thinking, she pushed forward and brought her knee up hard. He hit the floor with a scream so high-pitched it came out more like a squeak before he curled into a ball. Thanks to her brothers' endless roughhousing, she'd learned that little trick a long time ago. She grinned and stepped over his body, heading toward the large red satin curtain separating the back of the room. He'd think twice before placing a hand on her again.

A long string of breathy curses came from the man.

Then again, she'd better find Jack quick before the man recovered.

Pausing for a second to regain her composure, she then fisted the soft material, yanking it across the pole, making the large metal rings clank.

With a gasp, her chin dropped, and she stared, mouth open.

Stretched out on a recliner, head shaved, broad chest bare, jeans and black underwear around one ankle with a large smirk on his face, was Jack Drago.

Pure alpha sexiness just like she remembered.

A few seconds slipped by before she became conscious a shapely blonde sat between his legs with her head bent over his groin.

Face hot, she snapped her mouth shut. Katerina took a step back but hesitated, squashing the desire to turn and run. She needed his help, and she couldn't put it off any longer. She inhaled deeply and forced her gaze to meet his, not caring about whatever she intruded on. Light blue eyes examined her with lazy, licentious interest. Heat travel down her neck straight to the butterflies in her stomach. No matter how uncomfortable his stare made her feel, she refused to look away.

The man was still as gorgeous as she remembered with his grid-defined abs and huge muscled arms on full display. Some type of Celtic design covered one shoulder to wrist. Piercings through his nipples, one brow, and a loop in his lip made him look like a pagan god while the woman worshiped his...staff?

The warmth across her face and neck ratcheted up a notch.

"Hey, you look familiar," he said in the deep gruff voice she remembered. "I know." He lifted a stubborn chin. "You're that Savalas girl. Kristina. No. Katerina. Yeah, that's it." He slung a beefy arm over his head; his relaxed pose displayed muscles and toned body like a romance novel cover. "Come over and tell me how she's doing. She claims to be a pro at it, but I think I'm her first." He chuckled as he lifted a bottle of Devil's Cut in his other hand and guzzled a third of it.

Shaking her head, Katerina held up a palm. "No, no. I'll pass. I didn't mean to interrupt."

The blonde huffed and leaned back. "I've been doing this for ten years, and I'm a hell of lot better at it than the fellow in Atlanta you were telling me about."

Fellow? Eyebrows raised, her gaze returned to his face. He swung both ways? Then a mechanical humming stopped. What in the world? Unable to resist any longer, she peeked over the blonde's shoulder.

She breathed a sigh of relief on seeing the artwork the woman worked on. Feeling a little stupid—it *was* a tattoo shop—she eyed the design.

On the left side of Jack's groin, a large black ink pattern

depicted a fallen angel with wings curled over a bowed head and around a bruised, bloody body. Dark feathers brushed Jack's abs and ended where his thigh and torso met. The design was beautiful and poignant.

When Jack's cock twitched, she realized where her gaze had drifted, and her face heated again until it probably looked like an overripe tomato.

She twirled around, giving him her back. "Uh...I need to talk with you. After you pull up your pants." The image of his cock would be seared on her brain for the rest of her life.

Sure, she'd seen the male species in their altogether—her brothers lacked the modesty gene as kids—sick!—and she enjoyed the occasional picture on the Internet. For that matter, she was no twenty-six-year-old virgin, but Jack was different. First, her interest in him was in no way sisterly—nasty!—and second, he looked ten times better than anything on the Internet or any of the men she'd dated. Jack was a mature man, with muscles and tats bulging and rippling in places she never imagined could exist in real life. Oh, yes. The man was sin incarnate. And dangerous.

That was part of the reason she needed him.

"What are you doing here, sweetheart?" Jack needed her out of there quick. Even embarrassment hadn't made her leave. The way her dark brown eyes examined every hard inch of him, he expected to explode any second.

For the last week, while the blonde did some finishing touches to the tat, he'd handled the sensitive location without a problem. The artist looked mighty fine but with her husband keeping an eye out in the other room, he didn't dare touch. Truth be told, the blonde hadn't interested him, so controlling his urges had been easy. But as soon as his vision focused on Katerina Savalas, he hardened like a shore-deprived sailor spotting a titty bar.

"I need your services." She turned to face him. He liked her girl-next-door looks that included freckles across her nose.

"Services, eh?"

The first time he'd met her, she'd been rescued from a crazy human trafficker by the mercenary organization he worked for. The Circle normally didn't get involved in local problems, but the psycho had messed with one of their own, and they had no option but to stop it. Luckily for Katerina. After questioning her, he'd been ordered to return the sassy young woman to her father.

And her family wasn't the ordinary type. Katerina's father was the head of the infamous Savalas crime family. The Circle had connections on both sides of the legal fence, and to deliver her unharmed was a good opportunity to ensure the powerful man owed them big.

The only problem had been that when he tried to take her home, she refused to cooperate. Without a qualm, he'd tied her up and rolled her wiggling body inside a rug. When he'd delivered the present to her father, he held one end and gave a good tug. The spitting mad hellcat tumbled out at her father's feet like Cleopatra to Caesar. What could he say? He loved the classics.

He looked over her shoulder toward the front door. Except for the blonde's husband sitting on the floor rocking and holding his groin—he lifted an eyebrow at Katerina—he didn't see her brothers bursting through the door. The last thing he needed was for her no-holds-barred family to come after him.

After another sympathetic glance at the whimpering

man, he concluded she knew how to handle herself. So had she run away from home again?

He lifted the bottle of bourbon but hesitated, then set it back down. Maybe he'd heard her wrong.

"What services are you talking about? Where are your brothers?" He narrowed his eyes.

The blonde smeared ointment on the section she'd finished and slapped a bandage over it. Then she ignored them as she began cleaning her area.

"Can we go to Ed's Diner and talk about it? I'll pay." Katerina's gaze stayed on his face as he stood and pulled up his boxer briefs and jeans, adjusting his wayward cock.

Her cheeks turned a brighter pink. When was the last time he'd seen a woman blush—and not from anger?

"Sure. It'd do some good to get a little food on my stomach." When was the last time he ate? He remembered eating some chips last night. Or was that the night before? Drinking could do that to a person.

As he zipped and buttoned his pants, he continued to stare, looking for differences from the last time he'd seen her. She still had that roundness about her he liked. Women should be soft with some meat on their bones. The blond highlights in her brown chin-length hair looked real, obviously produced by the sun. The sprinkle of freckles across her cute nose confirmed her hours outside. With the small heart pendant on her necklace and dangling silver hearts from her ears, nothing shouted crime family princess. He'd never been interested in women like her, naive, stick-up-their-asses types.

What the hell was he thinking? The last thing he needed was trouble from the Savalas family. Yet, she looked at him as if she wanted to pour chocolate over his body and lick every inch.

No. To think of it, that was what he'd like to do with her. Certainly a good reason to stay away.

The most important reason to get rid of her fast was that if she hung around him long enough, she'd turn up dead.

They all did.

Chapter Two

Katerina had expected the man to be difficult, but to walk off and ignore her? *Rude ass.*

"I need to talk with you," she shouted at his back. Following him down the sidewalk until they reached the unlit parking lot, she stumbled and caught herself with a couple long strides. She hated the shorter days, and it didn't help that she was a tad night-blind.

He continued to walk in a drunken swagger. Somehow, he held his balance though there was no doubt the bottle in his hand had a short life.

"Go back to your daddy and crazy brothers. I don't need that kind of trouble." Without stopping, he lifted the bottle to his mouth and guzzled another third of the brown liquid.

"Mr. Drago, you need food on your stomach before someone finds you dead from alcohol poisoning." She'd never seen anyone drink like that and still stand. Her dad loved *ouzo* but he knew his limit. Probably a little higher than the normal man, but he and her brothers never appeared inebriated, louder maybe, but not sloppy.

Abruptly, he turned around and glared at her, pointing with the bottle as emphasis.

"You're not going to go away, are you?" Frustration apparent in his tone. Eyelids drifted half closed over beautiful light blue eyes.

"No," she said, crossing her arms.

He shook his head and turned, his long legs crossing the road before she could protest.

Did he really think he could get rid of her like that? Fighting the desire to throw up her hands and walk back to her car, she waited for his answer. She needed the man's talents. Big and deadly, he'd scare off anyone who tried to mess with her. Of the two most effective tactics that she knew grabbed a man's attention in a split second, she offered the second one. Besides, stripping on the street was out of the question, particularly for this man.

"Mr. Drago, how would you like to be a rich man?" He kept walking. She suppressed the urge to throw her purse at his broad back. "I know where the Elyton Federal gold's hidden."

He stopped and turned, narrowing his eyes as if he hadn't heard her correctly. "That's just a myth."

Everyone in the South knew about the Confederate gold shipment that had gone missing in Georgia toward the end of the Civil War. But the Elyton shipment had been Federal gold sent to the occupying Union troops in Alabama during Reconstruction. The details were murky, but half of the hundred thousand dollars' worth of gold coins shipped by wagon disappeared before arriving in Mobile. That was one point five million in current dollar rates. She imagined the gold itself was worth around one hundred eighty million. She took a deep breath. That was more money than she could ever imagine.

"Go with me to Ed's Diner, and I'll tell you how I know where it's hidden." She chewed on her lip. If he refused, what would she do? He was her last hope to survive the next few weeks.

"You're buying me dinner." He stared hard at her as if trying to read her mind. Then his forehead unwrinkled, and he threw a long leg over a sinister-looking motorcycle. It roared to life. Without waiting a second longer, she ran for her BMW. Thankfully, the signal light turned red as she sped toward him, giving her plenty of time to catch up. Then again, she half expected him to ignore the light and zoom through it.

Less than an hour later, Katerina shoved her plate to the side and watched the man wolf down his second hamburger. How did men do it? Her gaze traveled over the white T-shirt stretched tight across his chest. She already knew he didn't have an ounce of fat on him. And there he sat eating over four thousand calories of bread, meat, and fries washed down with beer. It wasn't fair. While she ate a grilled chicken breast with a salad and water, she endured another growl that sounded like *yum* when he bit into his meal. Was he half bear?

"You go ahead, Mr. Drago, and finish your food while I talk." She eyed him warily.

When she followed him the two miles to the diner, she'd been uncertain he'd make it. He'd swayed several times on his motorcycle and even crossed the double yellow lines. The man needed solid food on a stomach that probably had more bourbon in it in one day than she'd consumed in her whole life. She barely refrained from protesting as he ordered another beer. Maybe the food would sober him up before he straddled his . . . what did he call it? Oh, yeah, Harley-Davidson Night Rod Special. Whatever. He needed a clear head before going home. No matter how close that may be.

She breathed in deep and said, "I bought a few acres of land outside of town. In the center of it is an old antebellum-style house." She twisted the napkin in her lap. "About a week ago, while I was at the hardware store picking up some paint, someone broke into my home."

"Call the sheriff." He pushed the plate away and tilted his head back with the amber bottle to his mouth. His Adam's apple moved up and down. Then he set the empty bottle down with a thud and burped, long and loud. The smirk gave away his thoughts. He'd wanted her to be disgusted by his rudeness.

"I don't want to involve the locals," she said. She needed his help and there was no one else she would willingly ask.

He lifted a pierced eyebrow. "Why?"

"Partly, because if I were to find the gold, the government would take it from me."

"True. They're picky about someone claiming their gold but don't give a shit if you keep other people's, Ms. Salavas." He nodded and guzzled part of another beer the waitress had dropped off on her way to the next table. When his attention returned to her, he asked, "So you think you know where the gold is, and whoever broke in is looking for it too? Is it in your house?"

"Yes and no. They were looking for the map." Her gaze refused to move away from the gold loop attached to his masculine bottom lip. How would it feel if he kissed her? His smile became wider. She blinked and looked into his eyes. He was smirking again.

"What?" *Damn, does he know what I'm thinking?*

"You want *me* to believe *you* have a treasure map? I'm drunk, not stupid."

"Yep, a map with writing on it and a large X to mark the spot." For a couple seconds longer her mind refused to move away from that delectable pierced full lip. But then her bossy nature kicked in and she said without thinking, "You've got to be stupid to drink and ride a motorcycle. And how did you persuade the tattoo parlor to work on you while you're drunk? Do you how dangerous that is? Alcohol thins your blood."

"Money makes the difference, and like I'm worried about a little extra blood." He pushed away from the table and headed for the front door.

"Hey!" She threw down some cash and trailed behind him. "Where're you going?" When he ignored her, she said in a rush, "Okay! Your tattoos are none of my business. But I haven't finished telling you the details. I want to hire you as a bodyguard. No. I mean a security guard."

"Not interested." He slammed the door, rattling the glass. Ed started cussing behind the counter. Katerina grimaced and mouthed *sorry* before she ran out behind him.

A little breathless, trotting off to the side, she said, "I'll give you ten percent of the take."

"Ten percent of nothing is nothing." He lifted the helmet from the handlebar and slipped it on with the shield down, his eyes no longer visible. Could he still hear her? He straddled the snug seat and turned the key. Even if he could, the loud mufflers prevented any private conversation.

Hollering at the top of her lungs, she said, "I never thought one of the Drago brothers would be a coward."

The helmet turned her way. A chill traveled across her neck. Behind the dark visor, those eyes were likely telling her to go to hell.

She gave him the look back, adding, "I dare you."

Lifting one eyebrow, she rested hands on hips, elbows

out. He didn't have anything on her dad and brothers when it came to intimidation. He shut off the motor. She stepped back and swallowed deeply. Then again, her dad and brothers loved her and wouldn't intentionally do her bodily harm.

A quick glance confirmed the parking lot was empty of people. The faint bass from the diner's oldies playing in the dining room mixed with the wind rustling the leaves lining the street. The sounds reminded her she was alone with a dangerous man. And not just because Jack was drunk and a little angry.

"Coward, eh?" He slowly lifted the helmet off and returned it to the handlebars. "Now, why would you go and say that? All evening I've put up with you staring at me like I was either a triple-coated chocolate ice cream bar or a serial killer checking out his next prey. You really need to make up your mind." He moved into her space, towering over her. She backed up and continued to move away with each guttural spoken word.

The brick wall stopped her as its rough surface pressed against her shoulder blades and pulled at her hair.

"You're crazy." Or was *she* nuts for insisting on his help? He scared the hell out of her, and that was the reason he'd be perfect for the job. A wimpy guy wouldn't keep the bad guys away. "All I need is one week of your time. Isn't that worth nearly two million dollars?"

He lifted her by the upper arms until they were nose to nose. "Maybe I don't want the money." His gaze dropped to her mouth.

She gasped, her toes wiggled, no longer touching the cement. Her fingers dug into his forearms. His tongue darted out and licked the loop that fascinated her so much as he remained spellbound by her lips.

Oh, hell. She *really* wanted to know how it felt against hers.

He kissed her.

Her tongue licked the piece of gold. The metal was a lot warmer than she'd imagined. His taste shoved her straight over into insanity. Heat shot to her groin. She released her grip and wrapped her arms around his neck. Her hands slid over his shaved head, holding him in place. Their mouths vied for a deeper kiss. Every inch of her wanted to be wrapped around his tight body. He pressed his chest hard to hers, squeezing her against the wall. Her legs automatically separated and her ankles crossed at the small of his back. Her pussy rested just above his groin. She felt the tip of his hardness but not much more. The height difference, the way he held her, and their clothes prevented any in-depth contact, and there was no way she'd let go of his mouth; the man knew how to kiss.

Her fascination with Jack had started after she'd been rescued from a sex slaver. When Jack had questioned her. He'd been so strong and in command. Yet, she'd sensed sweetness behind that hard rock attitude. Later, when he'd rolled her up in the carpet, fighting and cussing him the whole way, he'd proven her wrong. She'd so wanted to cut his heart out. Despite the hatred she professed, her dreams about the big mercenary in the following months had revealed how much he'd fascinated her.

Yeah, she was nuts.

A car passed. The headlights shone on the wall nearby as Katerina and Jack moaned like animals, uncaring if they were seen.

Drawing long breaths, she let him go and pushed at his chest. "Let me down. We're outside where anyone can see us." Yes. She regained enough sense to care.

He licked between her breasts. Her blouse had come unbuttoned enough to expose her bra. Her nipples ached from their stiffness.

Holy hell, she never had anyone do that. It felt so good.

"No one will care. We're in the shadows." A broad hand cupped a breast.

"Please. Stop." She'd hate herself later. But would it be from stopping him or wishing she'd let him continue?

He released his breath in one long exhale and let her go.

Red faced, she stumbled. He reached out to steady her, but she regained her footing without help. What the hell was she thinking?

Thankfully, he'd listened to her. She kept her head down as she rebuttoned and straightened her blouse. She slapped at nonexistent dirt on her jeans in an effort to avoid his gaze.

"I'll take you up on your offer, but the money isn't enough," he said in a near growl.

"What? Are you kidding me? That kind of money could get me ten guys like you." As soon as it came out of her mouth, she wished each word would evaporate into the night air.

The pierced eyebrow lifted. "If that was true, you wouldn't be begging me to help you. You know I'm the only one who can protect and help you at the same time." That smirk she hated was back.

Beg? He only wished. The handsome devil. He was evil.

Her nipples and lady parts actually throbbed with that last sentiment. Not only nuts, but she was weird. She crossed her arms.

"So you don't want money. What will it take to get your help?" She avoided the dirty thought that entered her mind.

How would she answer if he asked for sex? Would she have the strength or will power to say no?

His look at her carried enough heat to send her up in flames. Was she about to get what she wanted from him plus more? Could she handle it? Him?

"I do want the money. That's certainly part of the deal. From what you've told me, there's no guarantee the gold will be found. So I could do all that work and end up, as I said, with nothing."

"And?" She hated sounding like a smartass, but she really wanted him to get to the point. It took all of her courage to stare into his knowing eyes.

He grinned and leaned forward, one hand resting on the wall behind her. Instead of trapped, she felt her body melting against his. Yeah. She wanted him. Badly. For months on end.

"Give me free access to your body for the next week and then if the deal goes tits up," his grin deepened, "we're even."

"Deal."

His eyebrows rose.

Did she just say that without hesitation? Why was she so happy to shock him?

Oh, Lord of Mercy, she'd lost her mind.

Chapter Three

"Oh, my God. Oh, my God."

She tried to stop the chant as they drove from the restaurant and headed toward her home. No matter how much she thought about backing out of the insane agreement, deep inside she knew she wouldn't. Their deal would help her in two ways. One, with him inside her home, the bad guys would think twice about breaking in. Two, with the man inside of her, she'd purge the fantasy out of her system and finally move on, forgetting he existed.

A glance in the mirror reassured her that he followed and hadn't lost control of his motorcycle. How in the world had he remained in one piece if he drank like that? He refused to ride with her, even after she offered to ask Ed to store the bike in a small shed behind the diner.

Jack insisted on going to her house that evening to check on the best way to secure the area. Tomorrow, he would pick up his few things and move in. His words. *Move in.*

Did he expect them to have sex tonight? Her heart picked up speed. She wanted it but not yet. Too soon. Probably tomorrow evening. She covered her mouth. What was she thinking?

Five miles outside of town, her BMW bounced along the long narrow dirt road to her house. The lights she'd left on helped to assure her everything was as she left it. She hoped.

The old clapboard house needed a paint job. Raw boards replaced rotten ones at various spots gave off an image of missing teeth. While the new roof flaunted what was yet to come. A lot of work still ahead of her, but it would be beautiful one day. When she found the money and started selling off the gold to different black market dealers, then she could afford to hire people to work on it.

Instead of parking in the back detached garage, she stopped a few feet from the porch that stretched across the front.

The roar of his motorcycle broke the silence as he pulled alongside her car. He swung a leg over and straightened. Then he stomped the ground. At first, she thought his foot had gone asleep. But when he pushed down the kickstand and steadied the Harley, she understood. He'd been checking the ground, ensuring it was hard enough to hold the weight.

He unstrapped his helmet, slipped it off, and hooked it on the handlebar as he stared at the house. His face and head glistened as he twisted at the waist, pecs and biceps shifting beneath his tight T-shirt. Reaching for the sky, he stretched and twisted some more, ending with a sigh as he rubbed the sweat off his bare head. The man certainly was fine-looking, all toned muscles and long form.

One eyebrow rose when he glanced her way. She looked down into her purse. Anything to hide her fascination with his body. Why was she hiding? Sure wasn't shyness. Maybe she felt uncomfortable with the raw need sailing through every inch of her body.

She scooped out the house keys and opened the large door. Grinning big, she took in the sweeping staircase. The house was only two stories, but the original owner had grand ideas, and though the stairs weren't wide, they gave the impression of a long curl across a woman's forehead, beautiful and smooth, providing the second floor a full balcony.

"Who's living with you?" Jack leaned against the doorjamb. Was he taking in the beauty of the stairway or too drunk to stand straight and focus his eyes?

"No one. I live alone."

"Humph."

Did he think if she had a husband or boyfriend she'd still need his help? Or accepted the second half of the deal? If her parents lived with her, guards would be everywhere protecting her. Then again, she'd still be under her dad's thumb. After their latest volatile argument, he'd kicked her out, and she was determined to make her own way and never go back. It was partly Jack's fault that she'd gone back home. He'd thought he'd been so cute tossing her at her dad's feet and claiming Mikolas Savalas owed Jack's organization. Oh, she knew about The Circle and their underhanded ways. Not that her dad was squeaky clean, but she didn't care. She wanted to be rich so as not to be obligated to a man again—not to family or to a studmuffin mercenary.

That little grunt he'd emitted she hadn't cared for at all. She was about to ask what he meant by it when she spotted the large camo duffel bag on the pine floor next to the door.

"Hey, little sis." Her brother, Phillip, walked into the foyer from the direction of the kitchen. In one hand, he held a large turkey leg to his mouth. She didn't have turkey in her fridge. Where did they both come from?

"What are you doing here?" She shook a finger at him.

Aware of Jack's every move, she sensed more than saw Jack push away from the door. He tried to step in front of her, but she held out her arm, hitting the hard abs she remembered admiring earlier that evening. Good thing he stopped. She wasn't sure if she could manage him and her brother.

"Can't we come and visit you?" He looked around with a frown. "This dump needs a lot of work." As if he just noticed Jack's presence, he asked, "Hey, when did you start hanging out with Circle scum?" His usual smile dissolved into a frown.

She ignored his question.

"We? Don't tell me Mister came with you." She didn't want Phillip there, no less his twin, Peter. When he was a kid, he'd acted so mature their parents referred to him as Mister Peter until they dropped his name. Phillip and Mister never went without the other.

"Well, actually—" Phillip stopped when Hector and Mister sauntered in. All three men eyed Jack with distaste.

Jack's height and build were equal to theirs, but he stood less of a chance against the united Savalas brothers. Three against one was never an even fight. And they weren't drunk like the swaying man beside her.

"Get your bags and leave. I don't need your help." She rested her hands on her hips. If she showed any weakness, they'd ignore every word she said.

"It looks like it to me," Hector said, sounding as if he wanted to snarl.

"I'm not leaving until he does." A scowl wrinkled Mister's forehead.

Ignoring her growing headache, she breathed in deep and said, "He's none of your business. I didn't ask for your help, and get it through your thick skulls, I don't want it."

"Aww, Katie. Don't be that way. You know we want what's best for you," Mister said.

"No. You want to get back in Dad's good graces. He's as mad at you as he is with me. I don't have time for this."

"Can't we wait to leave when it's daylight?" Phillip tried to compromise.

She almost gave in but she knew what would happen. They would be staying with her a week later, controlling her life as they did when she'd lived at home. And that was no life. Never able to go anywhere alone without them looking over her shoulder. Scaring off any chance of having a normal life, not counting they would take the gold and give it to Dad. They'd do about anything to be in Mikolas Savalas's good graces and be involved in his next scheme.

She loved her brothers, but more when it was from a distance. They were not referred to as alpha-holes by the women they dated for nothing.

"No. I said for you all to leave."

They started grumbling, eyeing Jack. Thankfully, he knew how to behave, either because he understood how explosive the situation could become, or he was too drunk to care about the insults her brothers tossed his way. Hector, the hothead, took exception to Jack's silence and reached out to grab Jack's left arm. That was all it took. In a smooth move, Jack swung a right and the fight was on.

"Stop! Dammit, leave him alone!" She knew better than to jump into the fray. The last time she tried to stop her brothers from fighting, she sported a black eye for a week. Instead of feeling sorry for her, they had teased her mercilessly.

The grunts and swearing continued. She had to admit Jack held his own until he tripped and landed beneath Hector with Phillip and Mister on top. For some reason, she sensed Jack reined in his temper so as not to hurt her brothers. Then again, each was a strong and capable man, and banded together, they were a power to be reckoned with. And really, how much pain was Jack feeling, considering he was probably numb from the whiskey and beer?

So she stood back and waited for it to end. She would have stopped it if someone had pulled a weapon. Or if someone broke a bone. Right. Having as many brothers as she did, she was used to it all.

A foot kicked out and knocked over a spindly legged table.

"You break a piece of my furniture, I'll shoot you!" Realizing it was about to get worse, she ordered, "Stop!"

The hopelessness of shouting became apparent as her brothers ignored her. They appeared determined to destroy her house and furniture. She'd just patched the holes and dents in the walls. They were crazy if they thought she'd stand by while they acted stupid. So she did the only thing she knew would draw their attention. She pulled the gun from her purse, opened the front door and fired it over her BMW into the trees beyond. The echo of the gun blast bounced around in the spacious foyer.

The fighting abruptly ended. A mixture of shock and confusion colored their faces.

"Now that I have your attention. The next three bullets to come out of my Beretta will be aimed at your asses. So you better have them out the door before I count to ten. One." She loved her brothers, but they knew she meant business. Each Christmas, Mister still showed everyone the scar he had on his thigh from when she threatened his butt last time. She hadn't actually shot him on purpose. The bullet had ricocheted.

God, she loved their sorry hides, but she was going to handle her problems on her own. If she wanted Jack's help and not theirs, that was her choice.

Tomorrow, she'd find the image funny, four six-foot-plus men scrambling off the floor, eyes and mouths wide open. They shook their heads, regaining their dignity, and glared at her and then at Jack. Phillip and Hector picked up their duffel bags from the shadowed hallway and Mister grabbed the one nearest the door. They glared at Jack after each bent to buss Katerina's cheek.

Mister stooped to stared into her eyes. "Are you sure this is what you want?" Always the level headed one of the brothers.

"Yes. We talked about this before. I need to handle all of this on my own."

He nodded and straightened. With a bear hug, he squeezed, released her, and then followed his brothers.

When Jack ambled past her out the front door, she said, "Not you, doofus. You and I have to talk first."

Watching him wrestle with her brothers...well, it made her realize he wasn't as scary as she originally felt.

He hesitated and looked at the brothers heading around to the back of the house, probably where their vehicle was parked. "But you said—"

She shook her head. "They weren't invited. You were."

Nodding, he stuck out his lower lip and rubbed his chin. She wasn't sure if it was a good thing to be alone with him, especially as he appeared to be on the sober side. She could handle the flirty, inebriated Jack, but the sober one...that was a different matter entirely. The all-business, deadly one she remembered from the time he manhandled her and rolled her up in a rug was unpredictable.

Shaking her head to clear it from explicit images of a near naked Jack that flashed through her mind, she stepped out on the front porch and waited.

First, she needed to make sure her brothers left. Coming from behind the house, two beams of light shone into the trees and then a large black SUV came into sight. The horn beeped, and the car slowly made its way down the dirt drive back to the county road.

Katerina slammed the door shut and clicked the lock. With the ease of familiarity she flipped the safety on her Beretta and dropped it into her purse. Her hands felt shaky but she was happy to see they appeared steady.

"Remind me to never argue with you, especially if your purse is within arm's reach," he said as he shouldered the blood trickling from a cut near his eye.

"Come on and I'll take care of that." She picked up the turkey leg off the floor and walked down the hallway toward the kitchen.

As she reached the tall garbage can, she tossed in the leg, then turned around and jumped. He stood inches from her. How could such a big man not make a board creak?

"Stand back. You startled me," she said. Her hand over her racing heart.

"Then we're even. You scare the hell out of me. I'm certain that you won't kill your brothers, but I'm fair game."

She chuckled and opened a bottom cabinet, pulling out a white box with a red cross on top. "Everyone in my family has been shot at least once. We're trained in self-defense and anything else we need to protect ourselves. With four brothers, I learned quickly that if I wanted to survive, I'd better be as good if not better than they were. They may have strength and size on me, but I can outshoot every one of them, be it with a gun or bow."

"Bow, eh? And four brothers?"

Unsurprised that he caught that. Not many people knew about her youngest brother.

She said in an even, stiff voice, "Cyrus served our country and died in Iraq." Her heart still hurt whenever she spoke his name or thought of him. He'd been closest in age to her. She loved all her brothers, but Cyrus had been her favorite: kind, generous, and able to kick butt like no one she'd ever met.

She pointed to a chair. "Sit there."

Once he eased down, she soaked a bandage with some hydrogen peroxide and patted the cut.

"Ouch." He jerked his head to the side and glared.

"You big baby. That doesn't burn." He continued to give her the side eye. "Not much," she admitted with a grin.

She sure did like his eyes, such a pale blue with dark rings at the outer edges. Strangely, she thought of a husky she owned when she was a kid. Would Jack nip at her in playfulness too? She turned away as heat swept over her face. No need to have Jack questioning her about the blush.

"How did you know they were here?" That would explain his question about living alone when she opened the door.

"You don't seem like the camo type girl."

He'd eyed her brother's duffel bag before she had.

"True." She nodded absentmindedly as she peeled the backing from an adhesive bandage.

A little more in control, she tried to place a Band-Aid over the cut, but he grimaced and leaned away.

"No need. It stopped bleeding." He stood causing her to step back. She wasn't afraid, just uneasy when his eyebrow with the loop lifted as he smirked. Obviously, a signature look of his. "Let me scope out the place. You said no one tries to break in while you're here." She nodded. He continued, "They've done so only while you're away. I'll make sure your house is locked up tight. Then I'll leave. I'll be back in the morning with my stuff."

She glanced at the numerous bags of groceries and dirty dishes and pans. "From the look of my kitchen, my brothers made themselves at home while I was gone. That should confuse the thieves if they're watching the house."

"Your brothers knew about the trouble you've been having?"

"No." If she had told them, they wouldn't have left.

She glanced out the window over the sink. Besides her reflection in the glass, it was pitch black outside. Even with the light on in the kitchen, the darkness made the house smaller and more intimate. His presence filled the room.

"I don't like leaving you alone. But I need to get my gear. For now, I'll check the windows and doors. Do you have a cell phone?"

She bit her lip for a second, swallowing the smart-alecky words that almost left her mouth. She reached into her purse and pulled out her phone to show him.

At the same time, Jack leaned back and flinched.

"What?" She really didn't understand the man.

"By the look on your face, you could've changed your mind about shooting me." He held out a hand.

She rolled her eyes and ignored his comment. He wasn't too far off from what had crossed her mind. "Why do you need my phone?"

Typing in a code, she unlocked the phone's screen. When he remained quiet she looked up. He closed his hand and dropped it to his side. His intense stare stopped her breath for a second. The image of a hungry wolf watching prey gave her a chill. His primal attitude frightened and fascinated her at the same time. She raised her eyebrows, pretending that his attention didn't cause her to feel restless. And horny.

"Put this in there," he said and rattled off his phone number.

At least, she assumed it was his. Before hitting save, she keyed in the name Spike. That had been her husky's name. When he'd been a pup, his hair stuck out every which-a-way. Though Jack didn't have the hair, those fascinating eyes sparked the comparison.

"Got it." She slid her phone onto the table and pointed to the backdoor in the kitchen. "There are also two side doors."

As she followed his path from door to door and each bank of windows, he appeared more sober. Maybe she was right, the short fight with her brothers had helped. She did enjoy looking at him. The loops and the tattoos on his arm along with the shaved head gave him a badass vibe. Even in certain light, a five-o'clock shadow appeared on his face and the top of his head. So he did have a solid head of hair. She wondered why he preferred being bald.

His long legs covered the main floor quickly. He reached the stairs and strode up the steps, two at a time. The first two bedrooms were guest rooms with a shared bath in between. He looked inside and checked the windows, even opening the closets and looking under the beds. Then they headed toward the end of the balcony. Double doors led into the large master suite. She loved that bedroom with the expansive bay window. The living room below had a matching one as the outside had a small turret on the back.

She shoved opened the doors and walked in with Jack directly behind her.

Jack stared in horror. He said under his breath, "What the fuck?"

Once he cleared his throat, he asked, "So you like white cats wearing clothes and bows on their heads?"

He'd heard of single women becoming a cat ladies, but what was this woman's problem? A wall of shelves held miniature ones, big ones, scary ones, stuffed ones and plastic ones. That was more than a simple clowder. It was a fucking horde.

"Actually, they're little girls dressed up in cat costumes. Hello Kitty. That's what they're called." She glared and pointed a finger. "Don't make another comment."

He raised his hands. "Hey, I own a real cat."

"Sure." She shook her head and pointed to the hallway. "Go. Leave. Lock the door behind you."

He glanced around, relieved to see no stuffed creatures on her bed though one sat on the nightstand. He'd be damned before he slept with dolls.

"Maybe I should stay," he said. The place was so old and needing repair, it wouldn't take but a strong shoulder to bust in. "I could help you set up some traps. That should slow down whoever is breaking in."

"No need. I bought a couple of Berettas at the local gun store. With the usual small town grapevine, chances are everyone has heard I'm armed. As I told you earlier, they're smart enough not to try anything while I'm here."

She had a point, though he'd feel better if she'd let him set a couple at the weaker locations. A lot could happen before he was back by daybreak. He checked the time on his phone. Only a few short hours.

"I'll return in the morning. Be sure to make room in your closet for my stuff."

"You can sleep in one of the guest rooms. When you return, pick one."

"I pick this one." He stepped closer, towering over her. Her dark gaze flickered across his chest. *Yeah, check me out, girl. You belong to me.*

He fought the desire to yank her body to his and rub every soft inch she hid beneath those baggy clothes. Faster he left, the faster he could return.

"You know what I meant. The one on the far side of the bathroom, near the top of the stairs, would do perfectly." Ducking her head, she fiddled with the stuffed cat on her nightstand.

"Princess, I'm sharing your bed and you sleep in here. So do I. That's the deal." Her bravado one moment and shyness the next kept his head spinning. He liked it. She was what some people in the old days would call a gutsy broad. Yet, she had a streak of femininity that tempted him to wrap her in his arms and do everything possible to protect her.

Hands on her hips, she said, "I—"

His eyes narrowed in warning as he interrupted, "Don't even think about backing out of our arrangement. I remember every word. Despite what you think." Unable to resist, he cupped the side of her head and ran a hand down her hair alongside her face, ending with pressing a crooked finger beneath her chin.

"But—"

Ignoring her, he interrupted again. "I'll be back when the sun comes up. Be ready."

Grinning down at her, he lightly pinched her chin. Maybe another kiss would sweeten her attitude. If there ever was a woman who needed to be fucked hard and often, it was the one standing in front of him.

She stepped back and glared, crossing her arms. He had no idea what went on in her devious feline brain, but he looked forward to knocking heads with her.

When he'd realized she'd shot the gun, he'd gotten so hard he'd been lucky her brothers hadn't noticed. Otherwise, they would never be left alone. He liked his women mean and dangerous. His track record had proven that. They needed to be to survive being at his side. The kind and harmless ones died.

He squeezed his eyes shut for a couple seconds.

Time to head back to his apartment. He needed a shower and a long swallow of bourbon. His head ached like a son of a bitch, and it didn't help having it slammed against the floor by the assholes she called brothers. That would sober up a man in a hurry. Hell, why couldn't she be an only child? Of course, then he would have to deal with her dad, and that was where the boys had gotten their bad tempers.

Without looking back, he felt her staring a hole between his shoulders. He sauntered down the staircase. Good thing he hadn't kissed her again. If he had, he wouldn't be leaving.

Checking the front door, making sure it locked properly, he listened to her shoot the dead bolt home. He stood on the porch and looked around. The quarter moon and bright stars helped somewhat to light up the area, but a couple motion sensors on the security lights did the trick even better. The trees to the right were shorter and younger. At one time there had been a field. The other side of the house had tall, thick trees. The place hadn't been a farm in a really long time. Off in the woods he heard a hoot owl. Some distance away a dog barked. Sound carried out in the country. So the animal could be on the next farm miles away.

He straddled the Harley and pressed the ignition. It started with a loud growl in the night. Lifting his helmet, he glanced back at the old house again. She'd been so proud of the monstrosity. Yet, there was not one room that didn't need an overhaul to ensure it was up to even general safety codes. It would take a fortune.

Why did she bother? Her family could build her a new home in the same spot.

Crazy ass family.

One thing was sure, he knew all about fucked-up families. He ran his hand over his head, feeling the stubble before pulling on the helmet with the sun shade and shield open. Time to leave.

With a snort, he turned his Harley and pointed it down the dirt drive. The rumble of his bike soothed his aches. He was happy her brothers hadn't messed with his ride. Katerina—

Such a foreign-sounding name. The name didn't suit her. She looked like an all-American girl with her freckles and soft curves. What had her brother called her? Katie. He liked that, but Kat sounded better. The woman had claws, but was still soft as a newborn kitten.

Once he hit the asphalt, he gassed his motorcycle and headed back to Sand City. A cold knot in his gut—not from the alcohol he'd downed all day—told him not to waste any time. The woman had stirred up a hornets' nest. He needed to head back as soon as possible and set up traps.

He tried his best to convince himself that his rush had nothing to do with wanting more of what he tasted in the parking lot.

Chapter Four

Katerina stared at the ceiling, watching the shadows crawl to the other side. Going to sleep would be such a good idea. For the first time since moving into the big rambling house, every creak and groan caused her to jump. Despite what she'd told Jack, she worried about someone breaking in, even with her there. Blast that man. Jack's paranoia was catching. So maybe she should arrange a few traps to hinder a burglar, but she knew better than most they wouldn't stop a person determined to get inside.

She turned on her side. The empty side of the bed taunted her. She ran her hand over the cool sheet. Which side did Jack prefer? Her heartbeat picked up. She wanted him but not inebriated. She wanted him aware of everything said and done. He needed to understand that. If he said no, then she'd be back to square one, unless she persuaded him to be her security guard without the benefits.

A grin spread across her face. She'd had several lovers after reaching eighteen, despite her dad's and brothers' attempts to keep her virginal. Being a Savalas, she was as stubborn as the men and proved it time and time again. Which was why she lived in a house by herself and forbidden to return home until she fell in with her dad's plans. His plans mainly centered on her marrying a good Greek boy he would find for her.

Geez! Her dad's choice was no choice. Who said she had to marry anyway? And why couldn't her mother take her side for once? Maria Savalas said only that she wanted grandchildren and wanted them all born in wedlock. They were so old-fashioned, it drove her nuts. They hadn't always been so provincial; she'd seen the pictures. Her dad had even told her they once traveled around and lived on love. Along their way to becoming middle aged, they forgot how to have fun.

The tinkling of broken glass jarred her to a sitting position in the middle of her bed, listening for more sounds. She slipped her handgun from beneath a pillow and rushed over to the double doors, tiptoeing on cool floors. Not caring that she wore only an oversized Hello Kitty T-shirt with matching pajama bottoms, she carefully opened the left side and listened for more noise. Whispering drifted up to her. More than one burglar had entered downstairs, and obviously brains were not passed on in their families.

Never break into a house when the owner is still there, and never announce it by allowing broken glass to hit the floor or talking while in the middle of a crime.

Over the years, she'd listened to her cousins and learned how to hot-wire old cars—the newer ones were a little more complicated—and how to break into homes. Not one branch of the family made a living totally legally. Through there were murmurs that one cousin was a cop.

Her brothers wouldn't return so quickly or damage her

home. No way would it be Jack. From the way he'd looked at her, he planned to come back alone. Besides, the man had no friends from what she'd heard.

Katerina flicked off the safety on her gun and dashed across the balcony to the top of the staircase, pressing her shoulders to the wall. Despite the glow from the arched window above the front door, that section of the steps remained in the shadows.

She could call 911, but by the time a deputy reached her home, she'd be dead or at the very least minus a treasure map. One of the drawbacks of living out in the country. Stopping the burglars was up to her. The next few moments would be a test of rubber meeting the road. Proof that she could survive on her own terms, with or without a man's help.

After each step down, she hesitated and touched the next one with her toes, not resting her full weight on her heels. Each assessment was done in the hope no creaks would give her away. As she came to the last two steps, she held one foot out and stopped. Those always squeaked—she'd been meaning to fix the loose boards—so she jumped, landing softly on the balls of her feet. The runner along the short hallway to the kitchen muffled her footsteps. She peeked into the open doorway.

A shiver of dread zipped through her when she noticed the starburst of missing glass in the backdoor's window. The hole was just enough space for someone to reach in and flip the bolt lock. If money hadn't been so tight, she'd had already found a way to change that door. More whispering reached her ears. They were in the dining room. Moving around the corner, she pressed on the swinging door enough to look through the crack.

Two men dressed in black clothes were carefully

peering behind pictures and pressing on sections of the wainscoting. They knew, or someone had told them, that the house had a secret room and tunnel. She would like to say it was for hiding slaves before moving them to freedom, but from what she was told, the house was built after the Civil War and the original owner traded in smuggled goods from Europe.

She really would hate to get blood on her recently painted walls and newly polished dining room floor. Why couldn't they be in the den? She hadn't worked on that room. *Oh, shit.* She was as bad as her family, thinking such cold, morbid thoughts. Then she spotted an old pottery vase one of her cousins had given her. No loss there. She'd always hated the dull brown thing.

Easing it off the cabinet by the handle, she lifted it high enough to knock out the nearest thief. Her plan was to keep the other one in control with the threat of being shot while she decided what to do next. She brought it down hard. The pottery crashed into the man's skull, but he remained standing. He turned, pressing a hand to his head as blood gushed out. At the same time, the other man charged in her direction. She lifted the gun and fired, hitting his leg. He dropped in his tracks, but the one with the gash in his head reached for her. Before she turned the gun in his direction, he snatched it from her hand. In a smooth, practiced move, she kicked out and the gun flew into the air and skidded out of sight beneath the dining room table and chairs. She ran to the other side of the table, throwing chairs in his path.

Though her skills in hand-to-hand combat were limited, she normally could handle most men. That was, if one at a time attacked. But what she spotted through the doorway scared her into panic mode. Two more men dressed in black hurried through the room determined to rescue their partners. Deep inside, she'd hoped she was wrong. With the large number of men involved, she had to face that this was no simple burglary for what little antiques and pitiful jewelry she owned. It confirmed it was for the damn map.

She dove under the table and came out the other side with the dropped gun in her hand.

"Just back away or I'll shoot." No way could she hold them off and survive until Jack returned.

"Bitch! Do you really think we'll let you get away with killing him?" The one with blood covering half his face edged closer to her.

"I shot him in the knee. He's alive." Scared but determined to face them down, she nodded over to the wounded man.

As if on cue, he groaned. Chances were high the guy would walk with a limp the rest of his life. He had probably fainted from the pain or hit his head on the floor.

Leaning against the long wall, she pressed one hand to the woodwork behind her, counted to the third bead, and pressed. A hidden panel slid open and she jumped through, slamming her hand against the release button inside. It quickly clicked shut, but it wouldn't hold them long, maybe twenty seconds tops. Arms stretched out in front of her in the pitch-black room, she felt her way to the other side. Thank goodness she'd left it empty. She found the groove in the panel on the far wall with trembling fingers and pressed. As the pounding on the wall behind her stopped, the other hidden door cracked open and musty air whipped by her, flattening the pajamas to her body. At the same time, she shouldered the door closed, then heard them shout in triumph.

Hoping the dark room would slow them down—*maybe none brought flashlights or would think about using their cigarette lighters or, shit! Cell phones*—she ran for the dappled light shining through the old iron gates at the end of the tunnel. The last door led to a tunnel and the outdoors. It had a dead bolt, but on the interior. Finally outside, she looked around for some way to wedge the gates closed. Then she remembered seeing the handle of a rusty shovel nearby. She jammed it through the old-fashioned loop handles. Then she ran down the path, jumping over dead fallen branches and tall clumps of grass. The exterior motion lights helped but made her easy to see too. She worked her way to the surrounding woods. Once she entered the tree line, maybe she'd be lucky enough to lose them.

Blinking, her *tad* of night-blindness slowing her down, she stayed on a small animal path that led to a stream. Trying to ignore the occasional sharp object pricking her feet, she veered off when she heard shouting. A few yards away she remembered a big patch of honeysuckle. She hated snakes, rats, and mosquitoes, but the way she felt then, they'd better watch out for her. She wasn't in the mood for any of their crap.

She dove into the vines and waited. The sweet scent of the yellow flowers brought back memories of playing in the Georgia woods with her brothers. They'd had a great childhood, roaming the mountain their family's compound covered. Who knew that all the hiding and seeking as a child would come in handy as an adult?

Despite her trembling, the rush of adrenaline helped her smile. Her family wasn't like others. That was a given. For sure, not like those she'd watched on TV when she was a kid. She, her brothers and her cousins were taught so many different skills by other family members, and many of those abilities could later get a person thrown into prison or killed. Having a dad who ran one of the largest crime families in the Southeast U. S. caused her numerous problems over the years. How could she bring friends into her house, where every room had stacks of boxes filled with stolen laptops and wide screen televisions?

The crunch of dry undergrowth alerted her. She raised her hand to cover her mouth to stop from whimpering. Her gun cracked her cheekbone. Biting her tongue in an attempt to hold back a cry—how stupid of her to forget she held it—she lifted her other hand and rubbed the tender area.

How did her brothers do stuff like this and make it look so easy? They had freaking nerves of steel. So not fair.

"Hey, asshole, let's get out of here. The bitch is probably a mile down the road. We don't have time for this shit!" The voice sounded familiar.

The vines she was hiding in shook. More from the "asshole" running to catch up with the other one than from her own fear, she hoped.

All around her the woods remained quiet while minutes passed, then slowly the sound of birds and insects chirping and buzzing picked up around her. That was when she felt creepy-crawly creatures dancing across her arms and down her back. She scrambled from the greenery and jumped around, shaking out her jammies and running her fingers through her hair.

"Off, off, off," she said under her breath while keeping in mind someone could be nearby expecting to catch her off guard.

Carefully, she zigzagged through the woods until she reached one side of her house. She checked for signs of the men. Any other time, when a visitor had taken the usual route up or down her drive, the automobile would creak and clank along the rutted dirt road, even waking her from a sound sleep. The trees grew too close together around the house. So with no vehicles parked near the house or along the drive, she guessed they had hidden ATVs somewhere further down the road and walked in.

Katerina hid behind a large oak, trying to decide when she should take a chance. If she went inside, and they waited for her, escaping a second time was doubtful. Or she could stay outside to wait for Jack's arrival. She hated the thought of depending on him to rescue her. But she was pragmatic. Her expertise in her dad's company had never been muscle. Hers was tied up in technology: from creating websites to working in the Deep Web. That was how she came across the house and map.

A year ago, while working on a problem for her dad, she had taken a break and looked for a house. She'd already started planning her escape from the family compound. When she keyed in her search, this house came up. It wasn't until she read about the gold and the missing map that she realized she was using the search engine she'd developed to surf her way through the unknown parts of the Internet called the Deep or Dark Web, as some referred to it because of its uses for known criminal activities. Conventional search engines skimmed the top ten percent, leaving so much more to explore. If a person wasn't careful where they poked around, they could have men in bulletproof vests with large letters written across their chests and backs come knocking on their doors. Or people much worse, like those who broke into her house.

Whoever had placed that information on the Internet, so deep, was no longer patient and had decided to come after her. Once Jack came to stay, she could concentrate on deciphering the map and hunting for the gold. Why couldn't men—it was always the male species—keep it simple and say, "The gold is found here!" With a big red arrow. No. They drew a map and put several different creatures and symbols on it and then added a poem by Percy Bysshe Shelley. She'd Googled that information. While she loved hearing people read poems, she'd never been good at understanding the lines. She was more of a straight-on girl. In this case, the poem was more like a riddle and she hated riddles.

Swiftly wake o'er the western wave,
Spirit of Night!
Out of the misty eastern cave,
Where, all the long and lone daylight,
Thou wovest dreams of joy and fear,
Which mark thee terrible and dear,—
Swift be thy flight!

No surprise she remembered it word for word. How many days had she scribbled and looked up meanings online with no clear results?

With a hiss, she kicked the tree and quickly remembered she didn't have any shoes on. Leaning against the trunk, she held her foot, cussing beneath her breath, and prayed she hadn't broken her big toe. She hated being barefoot outside and she hated freaking stupid treasure maps.

Chapter Five

Jack stepped out of his Silverado and hesitated near the truck's front end, keeping the thick engine block between him, the house, and anyone who might shoot. Who knew what mood Kat would be in?

The place appeared to be deserted. No birds chirped nearby. Something didn't feel right.

Not that anything looked different from last evening. Her car was still parked near the steps. He didn't see any new tire marks in the dirt and gravel.

Early morning sun reflected off the windows and exposed peeling paint beneath the eaves. The overgrown bushes near the long porch needed to go. Too easy for someone to hide behind and attack when entering the front door.

Kat could be in the back of the house and hadn't heard his truck pull up. He doubted she overslept. She wouldn't take a chance he would join her in bed.

A heavy sensation ran down his spine. Who was watching?

He stepped back and opened the crew door on his truck

and pulled out a sawed-off shotgun. In the South, it was the weapon of choice against thieves and burglars. Using rock salt, the spray would cover anyone heading his way with no worries about his aim, or killing anyone. Rather ironic considering the field of work he'd been in so long, but he was tired of people dying around him.

"Kat! Katerina!"

Out of the corner of his eye he saw movement. He swung the shotgun in the direction of the woods off. Kat limped out from behind a tree. After one more sweep of the area, he lowered the gun and jogged over.

"Out for an early morning walk? Got a blister?" He wanted to pick her up and carry her inside, but he knew how sensitive women were about —doing mental air quotes—being their own person. Funny, he hadn't realized how much he'd listened to his friend, Marie. Hell, it had been months since he'd talked to her. With her marrying the boss last year, there were a lot of roadblocks on that friendship. What did that say about him? That he had only two friends and one was a woman. Fuck it. He didn't need anybody.

"Not exactly." She limped past him in a dirt-smeared Hello Kitty oversized T-shirt and pants with a rip at the knee, and gave him a disgusted look as she continued up the steps. A pink-coated gun dangled from one scraped-up hand. He recognized the style to be a Smith & Wesson. But pink? Shit! Looked as if someone threw up Pepto-Bismol all over it. He'd bet money that she'd had it reworked with a bow-wearing cat on the handle. Fucking sacrilege. Where were the Berettas she purchased?

Kat stopped, bending over to rest her hands on her knees as if to catch her breath. Pain creased her forehead. "I had some visitors early this morning, before daybreak. I barely escaped and hid out in the woods until they left." With a deep inhale, she stood and marched up the steps.

"You're fucking kidding me!" He squeezed between her and the door. "Did they hurt you?" He searched for blood. If they touched one freckle on her cute little nose, he would give up his moratorium on murder and take new delight in it.

She tilted back her head until she looked into his eyes. "No. I'm smarter and quicker than they are. So get out of my way." She tried to push him to the side with a shoulder and elbow. He waited for her to realize he wasn't moving. She gave in and said, "I didn't know you had a truck. So when you drove up I ducked down and lost my balance. I checked. It's just a skinned knee and bruised ankle to go with a busted toe. Nothing to get all caveman over. Can you step to the side?"

"Let me check the house." With a hip check, he moved her hand from the doorknob, taking a chance she'd pull her gun. He didn't want to hurt her any more than she was already from her escapade in the woods.

"Okay." Raising her hands while still holding the gun, she wobbled back.

He clasped her elbow. No fight left in her? That caught him off guard. He lifted an eyebrow.

"What?" She jerked away and crossed her arms, staring with sudden interest at the woods. "I'm tired, dirty, and in no mood to argue."

"Maybe I need to find ways to keep you tired and dirty." Many positions came to mind. *Dammit!* He didn't need to be hard while making sure the bad guys were gone.

She gave him her usual look of disgust. He kind of expected it.

"Stay here and head for my truck if you hear anything."

He slowly opened the door and crept inside before glancing back. She was on his heels. He whispered, "What the hell do you think you're doing?"

"As I told you, I can take care of myself. You can be the scout, but I'm taking up the rear and coming in." Seeing her expression all serious and indignant, he had a hard time keeping a straight face.

He'd rather be the one taking her rear.

Hell! His dirty mind needed to stop. Later, he promised himself.

She eased over to a table near the door and pulled open a drawer. She slid her gun inside and pulled out a black Glock, and checked the magazine.

Relieved it was normal—the pink bothered him more than he wanted to admit—he asked, "How many of those do you have?"

"Let's say there isn't a room in the house without fire support." Her devious grin heated his blood more than he needed at the moment. Yeah. He needed to get that woman out of his system and fast.

"Fine. Stay a pace or more behind me. I don't want to swing around and knock you down." He took one step and she marched past him. With a quick eye roll toward the ceiling, he shook his head and followed. They stepped over a large puddle of blood near the dining room table. She revealed a hidden room and a damn underground tunnel. Why hadn't she shown those important details last night? Another entrance to protect. Was she not taking her safety seriously? How could he do his job she hired him to do, if he didn't know all of the house's secrets? It was bad enough he struggled to keep his gaze away from her delectable ass swaying before him. By the time, they reached upstairs, he wrestled with the urges to toss her on the floor, and strip those ugly pajamas off her and spank her ass and fuck it.

"It appears the men left, taking their wounded buddy with them," she said.

"Yeah." Jack almost had control of his wayward thoughts, but then he looked at the tangled bed covers. A king-size one. That would give them plenty of room to roll around on. *Damn!* He was even getting disgusted with himself.

"Jack?"

His attention gradually shifted over to her. The flush on her face warned he'd been staring for a while and had missed something. "What?"

"Have you been drinking this morning?"

"No. Not that it's any of your business. Why?" He liked seeing her all puffed-up and riled.

"You work for me now. So don't even think about drinking on the job."

He laughed and walked away. He better get out of there before he tossed her into the middle of that monster bed and did what they both needed. First, he had some business to take care of.

"I mean it." She huffed.

"Honey, I can drink and eat and fuck and still protect this place with one eye closed. Don't worry about me." Time to empty out his truck and settle in. Resting the shotgun on his shoulder, he trotted down the steps toward the front door.

"Do you talk that way to irritate me?" Kat glared over the railing.

"I do take pleasure in riling you." Flashing a grin, he turned and walked out.

As he reached the truck a furious screech echoed from

the house. Chuckling, he reached into the cab and started his new assignment.

Katerina jerked off her pajamas and pushed them down the laundry chute. The master bath had all the modern conveniences and was one of the few rooms that didn't need any work.

She loved her house, not only for its lurid history but because it was her first home, bought with money she'd earned. After graduating from college, she'd worked in one of her dad's legal businesses in their IT department. It wasn't until last year her dad had talked her into doing some of the Dark Web work for him. Family or not, she insisted that he pay her separately. He'd moaned and groaned about ungrateful kids, but his chest swelled up with pride. Yeah. She was a chip off the old block. Never do anything that wouldn't benefit the pocket.

After a long shower to calm her nerves and ensure all the critters were out of her hair and not nestled anywhere private, she checked her ankle. The swelling was down and hurt less. Only a round scrape remained on her knee, and her toe looked blue and deep red, but she'd survive. She shuddered with the thought of how close she'd come to being truly hurt and losing it all. Every bone in her body ached. Time for her to rest and catch up on sleep. Refusing to let her mind drift to the man downstairs, she wrapped up in a bathrobe and walked into the bedroom.

Piled in the middle of her bed was a long muscled, naked Jack Drago with his hands behind his head, propped up by pillows, and a sheet corner across his hips. Bruises on his torso testified that her brothers had caused more damage than Jack admitted. Considering the smirk on his face, he wasn't feeling any pain. Besides, in some perverted way he looked even more dangerous and so freaking sexy.

She stopped. Inhaling so deep, she felt lightheaded. *Oh, wow!* Was he out of some wet dream? Her knees were so weak she wobbled a little. The grin on his face warned he knew how he affected her.

"Darling, come hop into bed before you fall." He patted the mattress. *"Come, my sweet Kate; better once than never, for never too late."*

Oh, no. Oh, no. He quoted Shakespeare. How easily she could fall into bed with him. She never considered herself a highly sexed type of person, but he was temptation divine. And damn him, he quoted Shakespeare.

"I need to take a nap," she said. As if in a trance, she shuffled across the room. "Later. There are things downstairs I need to check on. You know, to see if the burglars damaged anything." She sounded as spacey as she felt. It had to be the adrenaline rush before dawn and the running, lots of running, before the break of day. Tired. That was why she felt so funny, goofy even. Just a couple inches away, her weak knees nearly touched the side of the bed.

He turned on his side and leaned toward her. Stupid sheet stayed in place. Cool air brushed down the center of her chest to her thighs. With one hand he'd pushed her bathrobe open.

And not one peep from herself in protest.

"Ah, sugar, you do look good enough to eat," he said with reverence.

Oh, hell. Yep. I'm going to hell.

She didn't care what time of day it was or how little she knew about the man, she wanted him. Terribly. Yet, she was so, so tired.

He scooted closer and wrapped an arm around her hips

and drew her against the side of the mattress. With an ease that took her breath away, he leaned over and ran his tongue across her mons, taking a second longer to dip between the tender lips before traveling up and swirling in her belly button.

"You taste as sweet as you look." His breath tickled her tender skin.

Before her brain could kick in, he pulled her down into his lap. His low chuckle sent shivers down the length of her body as he nuzzled a taut nipple.

He was Satan.

Why did she care? She knew she'd made a deal with the devil when she agreed to the payment. She wanted what he offered, his body to protect and to caress hers. Why fight it? Time for her to live a little and take a chance.

Without another thought, she shrugged off the robe and pushed at his chest. He cooperated by landing on his back. His self-satisfied chuckle ignored as she rose on her knees and brushed away the sheet and stared. In the tattoo parlor, she'd been too embarrassed to keep looking. Wrong place and wrong time to immerse herself in what he'd brazenly shown off. But nothing and no one was there to stop her from soaking in the erotic picture of tats, piercings and muscles before her. He was her most popular rub-one-off bad boy dream come true.

Then she yawned. She blushed and covered her mouth.

"You know, a guy could get his feelings hurt when a sexy woman looks at his naked body and yawns." His devilish grin brought a smile to her face. She traced his lower lip with her thumb.

He really was charming when he put forth the effort. She yawned again.

Both hands covered her warm cheeks. It had to stop.

His forehead wrinkled. "How early did those assholes wake you this morning?"

"Before dawn and it was late when I finally fell asleep."

He grinned and asked, "Had problems, did ya?" Almost blinded by his smile, she giggled.

"Too much excitement before bedtime," she said and bit back another giggle. Goodness, she always got the giggles when she was tired. Another long yawn. "Sorry." Every limb suddenly felt weighed down by gravity.

"Here. Stretch out, lie back." He arranged their bodies, her back to his chest. Instead of taking advantage of her weak state, he ensured that she felt protected by tightly covering her with the sheet, including tucking it between them.

"But—"

He pressed a callused finger to her lips. "Shh, rest. We have plenty of time."

A big tattooed arm settled over her waist and his hand nonchalantly cupped a breast. She gasped, more from how good it felt than from shock. She smiled and closed her eyes. In seconds, her body relaxed and the world disappeared.

Katerina cracked open her eyes. The slivers of light coming from the closed curtains indicated the sun was directly overhead. Then instantly she remembered the reason she felt cozy, warm, and secure. Jack's big body rested against her back with his cock pressed to her ass. Sure, material separated them, but she could feel his hard, hot length.

"Feeling better?" His husky voice shot a delightful streak of need to her groin. How did he do it with only two words?

"I feel human again." Her voice sounded raw. She turned over and pushed him to his back and straddled his upper thighs. She'd always been a morning person. Even if it was the middle of the day, her well-rested body thought otherwise.

His cock jerked as if he wanted her touch. Instead of giving it a good squeeze and pump like he probably hoped, she skimmed her hand along its length and then on to his well-defined abs. She delighted in the strength and firmness beneath her fingertips.

"Do you wake up like this every morning?" The awe in his voice almost had her laughing, but she held back. Their first time would most likely set a precedent, and he needed to know who was in charge.

He reached out and caressed her breasts. She slapped his hands away.

"No touching," she said and shook her finger at him. Then she wiggled her eyebrows. "For now."

"Yes, ma'am." He rested his shoulders against the pillows and waited for her next move. She'd been surprised he hadn't tried anything while she slept. The sweetness of him holding her for hours hadn't gone unnoticed.

He looked so delicious eyeing her with that hungry look and not trying to touch her again.

Unable to resist, she leaned over and tongued and tugged at the bars piercing each stiff small male nipple. His gasp sent heat swirling between her legs. Determined to take her time touching all the places she'd dreamed about, she pulled away and reined in her own hunger.

"You'll have to tell me why you decided on the angel." Wanting to tease him more, she traced one wing, relishing the way his skin quivered as she came closer to his stiffening cock.

"A sad tale better saved for another time. Touch me," he whispered dark and slow as molasses.

One finger traced a pulsing vein along his cock. She looked up and asked, "Do you taste as good as you look?"

Those beautiful blue eyes widened. He hadn't expected that question. Her grin had to be as devilish as his.

"You'll have to find out yourself," he said with a hint of pleading.

Oh, he recovered nicely.

Keeping her gaze on his face, she dipped down and lapped at the sensitive tip. He hissed as if he'd been burned. Yet, he felt like fiery steel. His cock was deliciously sizzling hot to the touch. She parted her lips and slowly lowered her mouth, tonguing every inch until she couldn't go any further. Carefully, she moved up as she sucked hard, and Jack's back bowed in an attempt to go further down her throat.

As if he couldn't handle it any longer, he clasped her shoulders, lifted her off his cock, and flipped their positions. Staring up into his face, she laughed.

"Why did you stop me? You taste as spicy as I had thought."

His only answer was a growl. Then his mouth covers hers. The rough kiss gradually slowed to a gentle test. Exploring what caused the other's heartbeat to speed up. Every time the loop on his bottom lip brushed her lip, she struggled for breath. His wicked persona pushed her to try everything she'd ever imagined doing. Her fingers pinched his nipples.

"Whoa, sugar. I do like your enthusiasm and don't mind a little pain, but blood can be a deal breaker."

A little embarrassed, she ducked and grinned. "Oops. Sorry."

He tilted her head up to look into her eyes. "I understand. I like knowing I make you forget yourself. Tug like this all you want." He placed her hands on his chest again and moved her hands up and down.

She sighed when he nibbled on her earlobe. His hands massaged and caressed, and every thirsty inch of her skin wanted more.

Jack found her mixture of innocence and wickedness to be a turn-on. Every moment with her so far had proven to be unpredictable and a challenge. And damn, he hadn't been this horny in years.

Not one inch of her would go untouched if he had anything to do with it. His hand glided over soft skin and edged toward the place he'd savored earlier.

"Little one! Where are you? I have a surprise for you!" The deep, accented voice echoed from the main floor.

"Dad?" The woman beneath Jack froze.

He flinched as if he'd been shot.

Chapter Six

"**S**hit!" That was the last thing he needed. "What's your dad doing here?" He ached so badly, wanting to sink into her, he had a problem concentrating on the ensuing danger.

Her wide-eyed look of horror warned it was an unexpected visit.

"I have no idea. Get off me!" She pushed and scrambled from the bed and disappeared behind a door that led into a walk-in closet.

If he didn't want Mikolas Savalas to shoot him where he lay naked in his daughter's bed, he'd better get dressed.

"Ah, hell." He shoved off and tenderly pulled on his jeans. Another shout echoed to the rafters as he thrust his arms into a T-shirt. The sound was better than standing beneath a cold shower. While he tied his boots, Kat shot out of the closet in a bright pink Hello Kitty shirt and matching shorts and headed downstairs.

He seriously needed to buy that girl a better wardrobe. About the time he'd reached the door, a green-eyed, white cat slinked into the room.

"There you are. What do you think? Plenty of room to roam around. Found any mice to play with?" He lifted the feline and started down the steps. Savalas might try to kill him, but Jack refused to hide upstairs or sneak out.

Petting his cat as it purred and exercised its claws on his T-shirt, Jack stopped near the front door. The foyer was empty. After peeking into the living and dining rooms for Kat and her father, he heard voices coming from the kitchen.

"So, this is what you spent your money on. With all the land surrounding it, you could tear it down and build a new one. Less trouble and upkeep." After glancing at the boarded-up pane on the backdoor Jack had taken care of earlier, Mikolas looked through the window above the sink and out over the patio into the large backyard beyond.

A big burly fellow with thick white hair and booming voice, Kat's father looked like Santa Claus sans beard with only a medium-sized gut. Despite his jolly, good-natured appearance, his treacherous personality filled the room, even darkening the corners. Jack betted he knew more about the man than his own daughter. Wherever Mikolas Savalas resided, even for a few minutes, he exuded death. How many had died by the old man's hands alone?

Jack looked over at Kat. No fear showed on her face. Caution maybe, but not fear. She stood at the other side of a large butcher block as if it offered protection from whatever her father would say next. Family could be hard to deal with even in the best of situations.

He winced. Every muscle ached, reminding him about the bruises her brothers left last night. He should be used to it. No different from the last time he'd seen his own brother. Rex had administered similar proof of how difficult family could be when they were disappointed and pissed.

Jack had been quiet, but Kat turned around and glared, jerking her head to one side, silently telling him to hide. When she realized he wasn't moving, she gave up, her attention falling to his arms.

"Whose kitty?"

"I told you I own one. Actually, considering she's a cat, she owns me."

Kat stared at him as if he'd stripped naked in the kitchen. Savalas remained next to the window as he stared at them with narrowed eyes.

"What?" Jack lifted the cat higher and nuzzled the fur. Perversely, he took pleasure from the disgusted look that crossed Savalas's face.

"You really own a cat?" She ran a hand down Kinky's back. The tips of her fingers grazed a nipple bar beneath his T-shirt. He swallowed a sharp inhale. What was she playing at in front of her father? Seeing the glint in her eyes, he fought the urge to snatch her up and kiss her. She asked, "What's her name?"

"Kinky."

"Go figure." Kat shook her head and then appeared to remember her father was in the room. "Dad, you remember Jack Drago."

"Drago." Mikolas nodded.

"Savalas."

"How's your brother?" The older man's eyes remained flat, but Jack understood the evil satisfaction behind them.

"Doing fine." Jack wanted to tell him to go to hell. The last time Savalas dealt with Rex, he'd stripped and hung his brother by the ankles. He had to admit, they'd been fortunate the old man hadn't done worse. Jack had seen the results of the old man's anger. It wasn't a gentle thing.

Silence.

Savalas stared at Jack, most likely waiting for an explanation of why he was in his daughter's house. He preferred that Kat explained. Yet, her slightly swollen lips appeared to be glued together and her father had a rep for being observant and impatient.

"Kat, Kinky is probably starving and all her food is still in the truck." Jack gave her his biggest smile. "You can find it behind the driver's seat."

She looked at him and then her father and back to Jack.

"You go and get it," she said. Her forehead wrinkled. She was so cute while confused and worried.

"Katie, that's no way to treat a guest in your home." Her father continued to watch Jack as he spoke. "I promise not to hurt him. Much."

"You two don't say a word until I get back." She shook a finger at her father and turned to leave, but stopped. Glaring from one to the other, she stopped at her father. "Don't touch him."

"Go. We'll be waiting for you." Jack jerked his head toward the door. Hey, had she just insulted him? For her to believe a man who had to be in his late fifties had the ability to hurt him...damn, she *had* insulted him. He sat Kinky on the floor and straightened, barely swallowing the yelp of pain. His back popped when he twisted.

Maybe she had a point. The bruises her brothers left ached like a son of a bitch. The bastards.

As soon as the front door clicked closed, Mikolas said, "I knew you would come sniffing around when she moved to Sand City." His gaze raked him with distaste. "That time you brought my daughter back to me, I saw the lust in your eyes."

"Actually, she came looking for me."

Mikolas's face turned red. "She's a good girl. When did

you become interested in unmarried and unattached women?"

Jack worked at holding the grin on his face. That was a low blow and the old man knew it, but strangely, it didn't disturb him. Mikolas wasn't the first to say it.

The front door slammed closed. The woman could move fast when she wanted.

"I'm back and you two better be talking nice." Kat walked into the kitchen, eyeing them as if she suspected they had divided up the silverware. She slowed and gradually made her way to the countertop near the electric can opener and set down the bag of canned cat food. Her gaze settled on Jack. "What did you say?"

He straightened his shoulders. "Me?"

Of course, she would believe he didn't know how to behave. When did it matter what she thought about him? But for some reason, he'd expected her to take his side. *Well, fuck!* She'd been licking his cock less than fifteen minutes ago. Besides, he hadn't been the one to kick her out of her home.

She studied him. When uncertainty darkened her face, he felt a stab of righteousness lift his chin.

"Okay," she finally said and turned to her dad. "Were you attacking my guest?"

Damn, that felt good. Pleased with her acceptance, he grinned.

"I only said the truth," Mikolas stated. "You don't know what you've invited into your home. He's a womanizer who thinks nothing of sleeping with another man's woman."

"Then I have nothing to worry about." One feminine eyebrow rose.

Jack's grin widened, and Mikolas caught it, glaring.

Her father threw up his hands. "He handled his last job

so sloppily he was assigned as punishment in the same nowhere town that witnessed his biggest failure. And if the rumors are right, he was fired last month for drunkenness."

"Truth be told, I was fired for calling my boss a cock-sucking, lying mother—" He stopped, checking on Kat. If her hands on her hips were a clue, it was best he halted his verbatim tirade. Although with older brothers she probably knew every curse word in existence, the manners his mom had hammered into his head came to the forefront. "Let's say, he understood how I felt about him and The Circle."

He sounded as if he didn't care, but he did. The Circle had been his whole life for over fifteen years, even when he and his brother had defected with the OS for a short time. The OS, Onyx Scepter, had been the heart of The Circle, its most elite and dangerous operatives.

"Just as well," Mikolas said, indicating there was more.

"What do you mean?" Kat beat him to the punch with the question.

"I heard they are having internal issues. Some of the West Coast offices are rebelling." The smirk on the old man's face irritated him more than he liked. Mikolas continued, "I say good riddance. They're a bunch of assholes who think they can interfere wherever they want."

"So other assholes like you can kill little kids with the guns they bring in?" Moving a step toward Mikolas, Jack clenched his fists.

No matter how much he hated and disagreed with the current Circle management, one fact was true. Decades of wrong needed to be corrected. The Circle was doing their best to change old mandates and habits, but just not fast enough to suit him.

"Whoa! I don't want my kitchen to become a war zone." Kat stepped between them, facing her dad, and pointed.

"Go home. Tell Mom to come with you next time. But wait for another month. Give me time to straighten out a few things."

"I'm not leaving until he does." Mikolas's cold eyes looked his way.

"He's staying." She crossed her arms. "I thought you said I needed to learn to live without your protection. You didn't say anything about me finding my own protection."

From the old man's expression, Jack could tell he would try a different strategy. Was the man clueless? The woman was strong willed and not easily controlled. He didn't know her well, but he already knew that. Hell, it turned him on.

"What? First, you refuse to date the men I bring to you. Yet you bring in this mongrel!"

"Ha! You didn't just want me to date them. You wanted me to marry one. I'm not from the old country. I'll marry whoever I want."

"You're marrying him?" Mikolas's incredulous expression said it all.

"No!" Kat shook her head vehemently.

"Fuck, no!" Jack said at the same time. Where in hell had the old man come up with that?

Kat looked his way. "You don't have to be ugly about it."

"We're in agreement. So what's the problem?" *Crazy woman.* He had to admit she was the type he imagined settling down with one day. Sexy. Big breasts. Bold. He liked a woman who wasn't afraid to stand her ground.

She snarled her nose and returned her attention to her dad. "Don't worry about me. I'm old enough to know how to handle him."

What the hell? He straightened. *No one handles me.* Visions of her over his lap, heart-shaped ass in the air, and him giving her a good spanking cheered him up.

Mikolas chuckled. "Good. It's better that way."

For a split second, he thought the old man agreed with him. When Mikolas walked across the kitchen toward where Jack stood in the doorway, Jack braced for a blow.

With whiskey-colored eyes scarily similar to his daughter's, Mikolas stopped and said in a low voice, so his daughter couldn't hear, "I don't like her staying out in the middle of nowhere. Keep an eye on her. Protect her. If you don't, what was done to your brother is nothing compared to what I plan for you." He leaned in a little closer. "You fail me, I'll have your balls with my eggs for breakfast the next day." Mikolas slapped him hard on the back and roared with laughter all the way to the front door.

The smile on Jack's face grew wider. Her father had just given him permission to stick close to his precious daughter.

Katerina pretended to ignore Jack as she picked up the cat rubbing her ankles. "Poor thing, probably starving."

Thank goodness her dad had left without further argument. What in the world had he whispered in Jack's ear? Knowing the old man, probably a threat.

Speaking of threat, she turned her back to the man with the wicked intentions in his gaze. True, she'd come close to having sex with him this morning, but the things her dad said got her to thinking. What was it Jack really saw in her? She wasn't an idiot. Most men would fuck any woman of a decent age and looks. He'd claimed he had no interest in money. But he didn't have a job. How had he been paying for room and board? Just didn't make sense. Then again, living with five men had taught her she'd never understand how their thought process worked. No matter how many times her brothers claimed that all men were simple creatures who wanted food, sex, a big screen TV, sex, beer and sex, and on occasion the reverse.

"We were interrupted." His deep voice almost melted her bones.

He obviously wanted the reverse.

She faced him, hoping to ward off his appeal until that evening. She needed the time to deal with her feelings toward him. In a way she wasn't sure if she liked him or not. He was arrogant, bossy, and dangerous. The piercings in his lip and brow warned her he was a rebel, and rebels incited trouble. Yet, they turned her bones to jelly.

He stepped closer, and all that male magnetism radiated from his body. He gazed into her eyes and a corner of his mouth lifted. *Lord, what a big sexy beast.* Her heart pounded faster, not from fear, but anticipation.

Breathless, she put out a hand and stopped his advance, his chest hard and warm beneath the T-shirt. "I noticed you had a couple boxes filled with your kitty's toys in your truck. My hands were too full earlier to pick them up. Go and get them while I feed her." Fire darted along her skin. He narrowed his eyes, not in anger, but trying to guess her motive. His thumb brushed her cheek. Her heart raced and her breath quickened. Then little pricks of pain shot across her torso as Kinky tried to climb over her breast to reach Jack. She understood the draw. She wanted to rub her body against his too.

"Kinky will be fine. She's probably full from your mice." His deep voice sounded like gravel mixed in.

What he said finally registered in her overheated brain. She jumped. "Mice!" Her head knocked against his chin. The cat landed on the floor and made a clean getaway, scampering off into the hallway. Jack grabbed her elbow with one hand as he rubbed the other where they collided.

"Don't tell me a woman who thinks nothing of holding off several burglars is afraid of a few rodents?" He chuckled.

She looked up. His broad grin shouted trouble. Dimples? *Oh, my God, he had dimples.* How had she missed them? Curling her fingers in an attempt to not trace the indentions, she struggled to regain her common sense. When he looked into her eyes and the grin changed to a smirk, it came to her. He wore that arrogant, knowing smile most of the time.

Wanting to change the subject from rats in her house, the small ones and the six-foot-plus one in front of her, she said, "That reminds me. We need to concentrate on securing the house. I don't want a replay of last night."

He stared into her eyes for a moment and though he didn't move away, she sensed his attention shift from her to what she said.

"Yeah. Time for you to show me the map." He stepped away.

"No."

Silence. He glared at her.

Ah, there he is. The cold mercenary she remembered from the first time they'd met. She shivered. Maybe in the back of her mind, she'd known that was the true Jack Drago. The one with the dimples was only what she wished he was like. When she'd walked into the tattoo parlor and found a drunk, teasing satyr, she'd wondered if she'd exaggerated the insensitive asshole who had forced her to return to her father under protest.

"Why the hell not?" His fists opened and closed by his sides.

Did she really know the man? Sure, he fascinated her

and she wanted his body. A blush burned her cheeks. She crossed her arms, not giving in to the urge to hide.

Despite how sexy he was with or without clothes, she needed to heed her dad and what her brain said. The man standing in front of her had worked for a psycho, no, make it two psychos. The first one had died under questionable circumstances, and she was perfectly fine in not knowing the details. His last boss, Ryker, scared the bejesus out of her with those scars on his face and black eye patch. Jack had done his bidding. True, it was hard to imagine Jack taking orders even though he'd voluntarily worked years for The Circle.

But still, something had changed about him from the last time she'd seen him. What? She tilted her head and stared at him. Then she saw it. Uncertainty. It flashed across his face. What had her dad said? *His biggest failure.* That was it. What had he done?

"What happened between you and The Circle? What did you do to be stuck out in the wilds of Alabama?" She personally didn't think it was a bad thing, but she imagined a thrill-seeking creature like him preferred tracking down terrorists or blowing up ammo dumps.

He stepped back again.

So he didn't like her asking those questions.

Strangely, knowing his kryptonite didn't empower her. Instead sadness weighed her down. For a man so sure of himself as to throw a kingpin's daughter at his feet without blinking an eye took a lot of guts. She wouldn't say he no longer had the balls for it. He'd already proven he did when he stood up to her dad minutes ago. No. It was that the man before her no longer had the heart to do more than shout back at a powerful and deadly man.

"Jack?" She eased closer, carefully as a person would a

hurt animal. The look on his face told her so much. He tried to hold his usual smirk, but it slipped, and she caught the trapped look in his eyes before he looked away. "Tell me," she said in a soft voice.

Chest rising and falling with increasing speed. Strong, masculine lips flattened. He fought an inner demon. Why hadn't she noticed before? He was running from his life. Staying with her was an easy way to not deal with whatever ate at him.

"Please," she pleaded.

"Sure. Why not? You'll hear about it at some time." He wiped his face, the stubble on his face rasping against his calluses in the quiet house. "I killed a good operative and friend of mine. Because of my arrogance, she died the worse way imaginable."

She? Had she meant so much to Jack? Was *friend* another way to say *lover*? Her chest tightened at the thought, a mixture of sympathy and jealously.

"How did she die?" She hated to ask, but she suspected he hadn't actually killed her but felt responsible for her death.

"Cave-in. She was there under my orders. The rocks kept falling." He squeezed his eyes shut as if he was seeing it happen again.

She pressed on though it hurt. "Was the cave unstable? Or did someone do something to cause it to fall in?"

Kat wanted to reach out and hug him, but he needed to tell her. She was certain he wasn't at fault. No matter how tough he acted, the man was a marshmallow inside. Sensitive people had to learn to toughen up the outside to protect the inside. He was one of them.

"A psycho had set a charge." His Adam's apple slid up and down as he swallowed deep.

"Did you know?" Deep inside, she already knew the answer.

"Stop. Just stop it, Kat. Nic depended on me to protect her. It was my failure to do my job that killed her."

"She's the angel. The tattoo. That's her, isn't it?"

"Yeah."

"Did you love her?" The pain in his face had her wishing she could swipe the words out of the air.

"Yeah. I loved her."

The tightening in her chest increased. A chill brushed her cheeks. What little blood remained in her brain helped to keep her upright. She wanted him and had for some time. Had she misunderstood his interest? Was she some sort of stand-in? Being truthful, he'd been right about how others could protect her. But she wanted *him*.

"Don't look at me like that. I loved her as *a friend*. She was under my command and I let her down. I let everyone down." He rubbed his shaved head and stared at the ceiling.

"Boo-hoo-hoo. You know, you're a real wanker at times." A tall rawboned man walked into the kitchen. His dark hair and hellish black eyes gave the crooked smile more of a wicked slant than a boyish one.

"Fuck you, asshole." Jack shook his head as if shaking off the last few intense minutes. "I should've left you hanging in that warehouse."

"Hey, wouldn't be the first time. You sure didn't help me when I almost rotted in a Circle cell. That lying rat bastard Savalas promised Theo certain merchandise if I disappeared for good."

"Who do you think got you transferred to a clinic? I had to wait until Theo lost interest in beating the shit out of you before I could arrange it." Jack glanced over before nodding her way. "Be careful what you say about Savalas in front of his daughter."

"What?" The man's soulless eyes looked into hers. "Excuse me. I'm Ty Roman. Your father and brothers and I have a long-standing agreement to hate each other." His gaze drifted down and returned to her face after a hesitation over her breasts. The crooked grin said that he relished the men's animosity.

She tried not to smile back, but she could tell his intentional rudeness was more to rile Jack than her, and he wasn't the first man she'd met who hated her dad and brothers. For that matter, Jack was probably part of that crowd. It was a burden she'd carried for most of her life. In the business of cheating people, her family had made many enemies.

The man's eyebrows rose in appreciation as he waited for her reaction to his declaration.

"You're bit of a rascal, Mr. Roman," she gave in and said.

"You don't know the half of it." His smile widened. "Please call me Ty."

Jack moved to her side. "Ty is not only a bounty hunter; he's one of the best at breaking riddles. You said the map had a riddle you couldn't piece together."

"Just how many people have you told?" She glared up to Jack. "And when did I tell you there was a riddle?"

"At the diner."

"I didn't say anything about not deciphering the riddle."

"Do you have the gold?"

"No. You know that." Frustration with his underhandedness had her close to screaming.

"You wouldn't want me here if you had already deciphered it."

"You have a point. Now about—"

"His share will come out of mine. Don't worry."

"I wasn't worried." She looked at Ty out of the corner of her eye. Arms crossed over his chest, he chuckled as he leaned against the kitchen counter, eyeing her and then Jack. "What's so funny?" she asked the man.

"You two. I've never seen Jack have such a hard time convincing a woman his way is the right one. They usually fall over themselves to please so they can suck on..." His eyes glinted. "...those little bars in his tits."

Face flushed, she ignored his crude teasing. "Well, I guess it's because this is my map, my house, and my gold. And truthfully, Jack and I were talking about—"

"Kat, we'll discuss it later," Jack broke in.

What was it with these men and not letting her talk?

"Quit interrupting me. I was about to say—"

"I think Jack was saying he was embarrassed by me showing up at such a personal moment." Ty shifted and crossed one ankle over the other, looking as if he planned to stay for the fireworks.

"Shut up, you stupid fuck," Jack shot at Ty. Then he moved in front of her, blocking her view of the bounty hunter. "Go and get the map."

Though his tone was harsh, the pleading in his gorgeous eyes struck her. He wanted the conversation to remain about the map. He had nothing to be ashamed of, but men were funny creatures. Emotions brought out feelings they were ill equipped to handle.

"Fine. I'll be back." She wasn't stupid. Obviously, finding her things to fetch while he talked about her was his modus operandi. Who was she to argue? She'd oblige one more time. Then they needed a long talk.

She headed toward her bedroom and the hiding place with her future stored inside. The time had come to show him the map and move forward, with or without him. A memory flash came to her of his desolated look. She tripped on the step, just catching herself. How could he fake such a heart-wrenching emotion? He'd been truthful to her. He'd cared for the woman and believed he was the cause of her death. What had happened?

Jack waited until she left the room. Once the creaking of the staircase confirmed she'd gone upstairs, he said, "What the hell are you doing here?"

"I thought I was your map expert."

"Riddle."

"What?"

"Never mind. Why are you here?" Why the hell were they such good friends? At that moment, he wanted to punch the man's teeth out.

"Ryker wanted me to make sure you're on track and didn't get lost in those lovely brown eyes of Ms. Savalas."

"I know how to do my fucking job without your help." Jack turned his back and pulled a couple beers out of the refrigerator, handing one to Ty.

"You've been off your game. That's part of the reason you're stuck out here."

"You know, I'm getting fucking tired of everyone reminding me of that." He knew better. He'd been sent to this little hole-in-the-wall town for two reasons. One was to get his head set straight. And the second was upstairs getting a bogus map. The whole house with the map in the Deep Internet was Ryker's bizarre scheme to hold something over Savalas through his weakest link, his daughter. Ty had been waiting for him last night when he'd returned to his motel room. He had news and the promise of forgiveness if all went as Ryker planned. Only thing was, the crazy bastard hadn't seen fit to tell him the real reason behind it.

"Okay. I'm glad to see that your temper has improved." Ty lifted the bottle to his lips.

Jack looked down the hallway, making sure she hadn't returned yet. "Tell Ryker the men he sent last night were unnecessary. I'm in without anyone the wiser."

Wiping his mouth, Ty lowered the beer. "What are you talking about? Ryker didn't send anyone last night."

"Shit!" That was the last thing he needed. Who else had she told about the map? Obviously, someone who believed it was real like she did. Breaking out in a cold sweat, his gaze darted to the ceiling in the direction of her bedroom. When he'd thought it was part of the setup, to frighten her into trusting him, he'd enjoyed the benefits, but how close had she come to dying that morning?

"Let yourself out and lock the door behind you." Jack raced for the stairs.

Chapter Seven

On her bed, Katerina gently spread out the map. It was the size of house plans, and the paper felt and looked like cloth. The black ink faded in several spots and spidered in others. Though it was crude, she recognized several landmarks: the mound of boulders near Rock Creek, the prehistorically large oak tree in the middle of a pine grove, and the long drive leading to the house.

The bedroom door slammed against the wall. Jack, framed by the entrance, stood staring at her. His chest heaved as if he'd hit the stairs at a run.

"What's wrong?" Her heart beat hard in answer to his wild look.

"You swear that you're not hurt?" Taking slow, measured steps toward her, he acted as if she'd dart out of sight.

"I've already answered that question." When he continued to glare, she said, "I'm fine. Quit looking at me like that. I was bringing the map for Ty to look at."

"Forget about Ty. We'll figure it out together." He came

closer. "Later. Much later." Grabbing a handful of hair, he pulled her head back and searched her face.

How sick was she? His roughness turned her on.

The heat and intensity of his gaze had her reaching for him. When he took possession of her mouth, a heat from deep inside her body surfaced with each thrust of his tongue. She ran her hands along his hips and thighs. Temptation nudged her fingers toward his zipper as she remembered what he'd done to her in the same position earlier that day. Before she could follow through, his jean-clad legs shoved her knees apart and he followed her down to the bed, pressing his massive body over hers. She sighed.

There was nothing like having a hard male body over hers, but Jack's solidness was more of everything: muscles, heat, thumping heartbeat, hard cock, the wonderful list went on. So it was time for her to explore other aspects she'd been craving and had only gotten a taste of that morning: the tattoos, the loop at the center of his full lower lip, the bars in his taut male nipples, and the delicious tangy flavor of a dangerous man.

She tugged at the bottom of his T-shirt, wanting help in removing it. He shifted and jerked it off and then concentrated on removing her top and shorts. Within seconds, they rested skin to skin.

It felt so good.

His large warm hand covered one of her butt cheeks. She loved how it reminded her how much bigger he was than her. Those fingers squeezed and dipped down from the back, causing her to tighten in nervousness before he reached the moisture waiting for his attention.

"Damn. You're so slick. Yes. I want you too, sugar." His mouth, mere inches from her ear, tickled the sensitive skin, sending a trembler through her body. "Don't be nervous. Anything I do to you will be what we both want. Right?" He didn't wait for an answer. "Whatever feels good. That's what we want." That deep voice rumbled as he added, "I've waited a long time for the feel of your heat wrapped around me."

Oh, my God! From head to toe she pulsated. How was that possible with his simple touch and blunt words?

"Quit talking and do it." Her husky voice revealed her eagerness. She sucked on his bottom lip, tonguing the loop. His long groan brought a matching one of her own. Her hands slid up and over his shaved head.

Yes! That turned her on more than she ever expected.

He clasped the sides of her head and kissed her properly. The man knew his business.

Her nipples hardened to painful points.

"Touch me more. Please," she pleaded. Where was her control from earlier that day? At that time, he'd been the one begging her to touch him. She only knew she needed this man on her and in her. Her skin screamed for his touch, aching for release from the tight, burning feeling spreading over her body.

He pushed her shoulders to the mattress and cupped her breasts. His large hands squeezed with the right pressure, nearly circling the mounds, as he pulled her nipples with thumb and forefinger. How did he know what she wanted? She gasped, taking in air that had left her body. She arched, silently begging for more. He kissed her with a gentle suck on her tongue as he pulled away and dipped in again.

His head fell back as he pumped his groin against hers, not entering but slipping between her slick folds. Whenever she tried to adjust her hips to take him inside, he moved slightly to grind once more. Frustration drove her to the edge of insanity.

She covered his hands with hers, stopping his sensual torture. Light blue eyes looked down into her face. "Please," she whispered.

Gentleness swept over the harsh lines of his brows and mouth.

What was he thinking to bring such a sweet look to his face?

Jack lifted his hips and eased into her warmth.

Coming home. No. It felt more than that. He knew with certainty, he belonged wrapped between her legs and cock-deep in the heart of her. No woman had ever made him feel so much. He wanted to savor every second.

The moon had risen and shone through the bay window. Distorted by the beveled glass, different shades of moonlight fell across the bed and her body.

With a deep breath, he softly recited, "*'Then look at me by moonlight, watch for me by moonlight, I'll come to thee by moonlight, though hell should bar the way.'*"

She undulated around his cock and tilted him toward the edge. He bit his tongue, regaining control.

"Oh, my God," she groaned. "Poetry. Who wrote that?"

"Alfred Noyes." He grinned down at her and thrust. "Do you really want to talk about him now?"

"Sorry." Her lips turned up in a sweet smile.

"It's you. I look at you, and the words come to back to me. Now, shut up," he teased. Unable to resist her delectable giggling mouth, he kissed her as he pulled back and thrust hard again and again. She was perfect, feminine and strong. Those damn freckles, they turned him on so much.

Her hands slid to his waist and fingernails dug in. She threw her head back and groaned, "Jack," and her body tightening and releasing again around his cock pushed him to his satisfaction.

He eased over to the side, keeping her clasped to his chest. As he pressed a kiss to the top of her head, soft honey-smelling strands tickled his nose. His cock still inside her throbbed.

Damn. He'd never get enough of her.

Strange, how other women faded in comparison. If he'd told his brother that, Rex would laugh in his face and call him a liar. But in all his life, he'd slept with less than ten different women. Jack was quite aware how people expected the worst from him. How many times had he protected those he cared about, only to be slapped in the face later? To hear from their lips how much he couldn't be trusted. Olivia, the woman he walked through hell for, Ryker, his former best friend, and his own brother all hated him. They'd never know how often he placed his body in the line of fire for their sakes. He'd never tell. It would be pointless. They wouldn't believe a word. They had no idea how loyal he was to those he cared for. That was why he had only two people he called friend. Marie and Ty had saved his life. More than once. And he'd never forget.

He lightly squeezed the woman in his arms. Who was he kidding? He was up shit creek without a paddle when Kat learned the truth. So, he'd keep her safe and when it was over, leave. Same old, same old. Chances were she wouldn't want anything to do with him when she found out he still worked for The Circle, and they had set her up.

Kat's breath tickled his chest. He leaned back a little.

She was asleep. She actually fell asleep while he held her. Had anyone ever felt that safe with him to do that? He couldn't remember.

He glanced up at the ceiling and blinked. *Damn.* He hated getting dust in his eyes.

Katerina woke up and immediately knew Jack was no longer in bed with her. In the dark, from the top shelf between her largest Hello Kitty dolls, two eerily greenish-yellow eyes blinked at her. A shiver ran down her back.

Jack continued to surprise her. He owned a cat, and he made no bones about loving the animal. And somehow, he held on to his temper with her dad and not many people could lay claim to that. The man knew how to touch her and bring her to climax faster than...herself.

Whoa! Was he for real?

Yes. Deep inside she felt he cared for her. But was it more than sex? Or was that hopeful wishing on her part? She'd been wanting him from the moment he wrapped her in a rug for her dad. Sure, she'd hated him for taking her back, but the man was a romantic.

She groaned and squeezed her eyes and thighs, remembering his low, deep voice reciting poetry. What man in the real world did that kind of stuff? Obviously, Jack did. If he read poems to her all day, she was certain she'd climax over and over again.

Even with his mouth shut, the way he touched her, he knew a woman's body, her body. Delightful shivers traveled down her torso as the remembered sensation of his thick cock sliding into her, filling her, stretching her to the limit.

Oh, yes, the man was hot.

In a sharp burst of memory, she could hear an old

boyfriend saying, "Why in the hell do you women equate good sex with love?"

Was that what she was doing? Hands over face, she moaned. What was wrong with her?

She was a Savalas. She never needed another person's help. That was why she moved out of the house. To prove to her dad she could survive without his help. Sure, she needed Jack's help in keeping the crazies away, but it was a temporary problem and a simple solution.

Man, oh, man.

She sighed and hugged herself. He was wonderful in bed, and she hoped that was only the beginning.

She sat up. Why was she reliving what she could experience again? Where was he? The night was still young.

Had he heard a noise and gone to investigate?

The map.

She scrambled for the light and looked around. At the foot of the bed, twisted in with the comforter, was the map. She stared at it.

Why hadn't he taken it? Most men like Jack would've stolen it and tried to decipher where the gold was hidden, keeping the gold for themselves. Was what Jack said true? He had plenty of money and was interested in only her body? That would be a first. All of her boyfriends had wanted to meet her dad, be part of the organization, be powerful and rich. Even the ones who had no idea the front businesses hid the illegal ones.

Then what was going on? Where was Jack?

She pulled on an oversized Hello Kitty T-shirt and black gym shorts and rushed downstairs. She grabbed a gun and took each step on her tiptoes as she listened for voices or other footsteps.

A dim light came from the kitchen. She found Jack

sitting at the table, bare chested, wearing jeans unsnapped but zipped up, staring at a half empty bottle of whiskey resting on its side.

"What are you doing?" Was he drunk? He had the look of a man with a lot weighing on his mind.

"Did you know that whiskey in an oak barrel can be as much as 190 proof? And most straight whiskies are 80 proof in the bottle. Yet this smooth son of a bitch," he gently set the empty bottle in front of him on its side, "is 90 proof." He twirled the bottle as if playing the old kissing game. "My dad gave me my first taste at the age of nine. He said it would put hair on my chest, make me a real man."

She cringed at his self-derisive laugh as she eased into the chair across from him.

Without lifting his gaze away from the bottle, he continued, "He worried Mom would turn us into pussies. His favorite word." Jack said in a rough drawl, "Y'all little bastards are nothing but pussies." A frown creased his forehead. "He beat on us often, especially Rex, until my brother hit a growth spurt at fourteen and shot up past Dad's five-six. Then he loved pitting me and Rex against each other. I don't know if you've ever met my brother, but I gave him the scar on his face. I threw a beer bottle at him." He twirled the bottle and muttered, "I truly thought he'd duck." Another twirl. "Blood went everywhere. Dad called him a whiny baby and refused to take him to the hospital." He shook his head. "Stitches would've helped minimize the scarring. I'm sure of it." His voice trailed off.

Doing her best, she tried not to show how horrified everything he said made her feel. Her dad could be a prime bastard, but he'd never physically hurt them or encouraged them to harm each other.

She planted an elbow on the table and lifted her wrist to

cover her mouth, waiting for more. She couldn't imagine Jack willing to share again. Whatever pushed him to repeat such memories to her, she had no idea, but he obviously felt it was important for her to know.

Silence darkened the room. Unable to take it any longer, she stood and walked around the table and kneeled next to his chair.

"Jack, we have no control over who are our parents. I'm a prime example of that. My dad has never been as cruel as yours, but he easily forgets that I'm not his pawn to control. A few months ago, he offered me as a bribe to a man he wanted to bring in as a partner. Sure, he expected the man to marry me. When he refused, Dad was furious that I refused to try to change the man's mind. I have a feeling if not for my brothers taking my side, I'd be married to a stranger now."

"What about your mother? What did she say?"

"She told me that I was being selfish. That I wasn't a boy and couldn't really contribute to the family business until I married."

"What the hell?" Outrage darkened his face.

Relieved that he felt the same way as she had, she said, "No matter how many times I say that they are old school, I still can't fully forgive them. But for Dad to come by to see me...well, that means he's possibly feeling some regret."

"Having only my asshole of a dad as an example, there's no way I'd trust him. Sorry, Kat, but your father is relentless in getting what he wants." Jack leaned over and gently brushed hair out of her eyes.

"See. I knew you would understand." She looked into his eyes. Again, she became hypnotized by the beautiful light blue with dark rings. Without thought, she slid her hand up his thigh. "Do you really want to talk about our parents right now?" She repeated nearly what he had said earlier.

When he shook his head, she grinned and dropped her attention to his lap. Her hand skimmed over his thigh and cupped the bulge growing next to the zipper. She loved playing with that part of his anatomy.

He shifted in his seat, stretching out his legs on each side of her, and leaned back in his chair. Eyelids lowered to half-mast, he watched her unzip his jeans. No underwear to stop her hand from wrapping around his length.

Men's bodies were such delicious contradictions: hairy and smooth, rigid and tender, and salty and sweet. With her gaze attached to his, she leaned down and licked the tip and then ran her tongue around the head. His sharp inhale brought a grin to her face. Yeah, she wanted him to harden every time he looked at her mouth in the future.

His cock lengthened and thickened more. She gave him a long, firm stroke.

In a slow drawn-out plea, he said, "Fuck."

"We've already done that. I want this now." With a dip of her head, she sucked in the tip and tongued the opening as she fisted the rest.

He yelled her name. From pleasure. The way she always preferred it. His fingers clasped her hair as he thrust up his hips. She swallowed more of his length but stopped additional inches from choking her by tightening her hand.

He untangled his hand to clutch her arm. Squeezing hard enough to force her release of his cock, he stood with her. She opened her mouth to protest, but stopped when she noticed his look. His hard determined stare betrayed how he'd forgotten his own strength; he didn't even realize his grip was uncomfortable.

Then he released her but only to jerk down her shorts,

shoving them the rest of the way off her hips. At the same time, she slipped off her T-shirt and tossed it to the side. His legs pressed between her knees. Then he pushed her shoulders until they touched the table. Her breasts rose and fell in excitement, drawing his attention to the hard tips for a moment before he leaned over her.

"*'One kiss, my bonny sweetheart, I'm after a prize tonight...'*" he whispered, tracing a finger from her belly button to the wetness hidden in her folds.

"There you go. Reciting again," she teased, certain a sappy grin showed on her face. Her voice raspy from being unable to pull in enough air.

Then she felt a hardness probing between her legs. Lifting her head, she watched as he eased into her. The slide of hot male had her gasping. *Yes.* She needed him again. Badly.

Each thrust shook her breasts and the table beneath her. She wanted more. As if he read her mind, his rough hands covered the stiff-tipped mounds and squeezed, lifted, pulled with mind-blowing results. How did he know that she'd enjoyed the hell of it? Her breasts felt as if they would burst from her skin in need.

Each plunge and massage caused her body to feel too much. When she came, she was certain she floated inches above the table. His big body rested lightly over hers. His elbows barely held his chest above hers.

They ended up on the floor pulling the linen tablecloth with them. The material prevented the cold slate floor from freezing their skin. Somewhere along the way, he'd shed his jeans. Both naked, immersed in caressing each other as they took turns cuddling and talking about their past. He told her the truth about his parents and the measures he took to protect his younger brother.

"You did what you had to do." Her understanding humbled him. He'd never told a living being his darkest secret for fear of being called an animal.

He glanced down to the woman in his arms. He loved her. There had to be a way to keep her in his life. When it was all over and the truth was finally out, he would do anything to make her understand. Beg. Plead. Whatever it took.

"It was too little too late," he admitted. He pressed her face to his chest, hoping she wouldn't see the tears in the corners of his eyes.

"Oh, I wouldn't say too little. You didn't know how to stop it before then. I wish things had been better for you and Rex, but it was because you rose above the cruelty of your father that you're a good man now. I will admit you do still have things you need to work on." She kissed his chest as he chuckled. "Yet, no matter, you're a good man, Jack Drago." She lifted her face and covered his mouth with hers. The kiss deepened as if she wanted to touch his soul. Dear sweet Jesus, she had. He'd die if anything ever happened to her.

The tinkling of broken glass hitting the floor pulled Jack's attention from the languid woman in his arms. "You got to be fucking kidding me," he growled and helped her to her feet.

"They've come back?" She craned her neck around, looking for the danger.

"Shh." He pressed a finger to her lips. Then he snatched his jeans from the floor, yanking them up with one hand as he reached with the other for his gun on the chair nearby.

"Let me check. Crawl under the table and stay out of the way."

"Yeah, right. Let me get another gun and I'll help. No way am I hiding." Without waiting for his answer, she pulled on her oversized T-shirt. It covered her delectable ass. She jogged over to a tall cabinet and opened it up. Instead of the expected plates and cups, the shelves were gone and hung from hooks were various weapons: a rifle, shotgun, and two pistols along with knives in graduated lengths from a dangerous pig sticker to a deadly machete.

He watched her pick out a thin knife, what some would call a stiletto, and exchange the gun she'd brought into the kitchen for a pistol that had a long magazine hanging from the grip, letting Jack know she would have more than twenty-four shots from that one.

Maybe she had more of her dad's genes than he felt comfortable with considering what they'd just done. Then again, he admitted that her self-sufficiency turned him on.

Chapter Eight

"This way," Katerina whispered to Jack, nodding toward a tall cabinet on the opposite wall.

She counted on whoever broke in last night —hard to believe it had been less than twenty-four hours— to head for the dining room and then the hidden room. They obviously didn't know the house.

With a hard push against one end, the cabinet slid away from the wall on recently greased ball bearings. Behind it was a recessed doorway. She opened it. A musky smell filtered into the kitchen.

Jack clasped her arm and leaned down to her ear. "How many secrets does this place have?" He looked inside the short hallway. She cupped the side of his face and smiled.

"I'll tell you later," she whispered and kissed his cheek.

During the few months she'd lived there, she'd found several hidden passageways. The man who built the place had obviously led a dangerous life or had mental issues. So far, the secret rooms and passageways had come in handy twice for her.

She tugged on the cabinet with Jack's help, and it glided

closed, sealing them in with a quiet click. In the small, narrow space, her shoulder touched his chest. Though pitch-black, instead of the suffocating feeling she expected, his big presence comforted.

"What next?"

Without answering she reached up and tugged on a rope. A cool breeze came through from the end of the tiny hallway, filling the area with a dank scent. She knew it was from an opening a couple yards away. Palm flat on the narrow door, she carefully pushed it the rest of the way open and ducked through, stepping to the side. Jack followed behind. She sensed he loomed over her, but he had enough sense not to go forward. If he had, and she hadn't caught him in time, he'd have tumbled down about thirty steps.

"Let's see if they found the entrance to the basement." She ran her hand over the wall until she reached into a depression and pulled out a flashlight. With flick of a finger, the circle of light pierced the darkness for about ten feet, not even showing the end of the staircase.

"Damn! How deep does it go?"

"Almost twenty feet. The old guy stored liquor in the steady temp. Probably a lot of it excise-tax-free."

"Why no lights?" Jack stayed two steps back, she guessed, so not to rush her and make her trip.

"Rats ate through a lot of the wiring in the house. I felt the living area was more important." They talked in a whisper, but she worried what they'd find below. She pressed a finger to her lips. "Shh."

She half expected Jack to reach for the flashlight when they hit bottom. He merely shifted to one side. He probably planned to dart in front of her if trouble popped up. With only footprints her size showing up on the dirty floor, her shoulders relaxed. They were alone. That was as alone as a person could be with rats scurrying over their feet. The large area was filled with numerous dusty, empty shelves waiting for wine bottles.

Lifting the flashlight until she could see down the middle aisle, a bolted door waited on the other end.

"We're good. That's the only way out or in here besides the stairs." She nodded.

"This is too easy," he said. His eyes narrowed as if he could see through the door.

"What do you mean?"

"From what you've told me, they've been watching you for some time. If it was me, I would know by now every inch of this place and have a guard at every exit."

"Actually, the door leads to another underground passage and on to the garage. Really it's rather neat. Between us and the garage, there's a handcar and rails for it to ride on. Makes moving barrels or crates of liquor in and out of the basement quick and painless." She jogged over to the end of a shelf and reached on her tiptoes to the top. The key waited in the same spot she'd left it. "Let's get out of here. We can circle back around and catch them." She wanted the trouble to end tonight. Enough was enough.

She unlocked the bolt and just as she pulled, Jack shouted something. A bright light blinded her and pain dropped her to the floor. Fingers dug into her arms and explosions surrounded her.

Sprawled on the floor, shouting from above, her eyes adjusted enough to see Jack beating the crap out of a man against the wall while two others pulled at his neck and upper arms.

"You son of a bitch! I told you not to touch her!" Jack

said each word with a punch to the man's face. "I followed his fucking orders!"

Jack had fucked up big time.

He wanted to stop. No, he needed to stop pummeling the man's face before he crushed his skull in, but the visual of the door throwing Kat back onto the floor and blood pouring from her nose sent him into overdrive.

Men grappled to gain control of his arms until they finally jerked him away and piled on top. They took his gun from the back of his pants.

"Jack! It's me. Stop it!" Ty stood over him, chest heaving. "We didn't know it was you and the girl."

"You stupid son of a bitch! What did you expect? She lives here!" His left cheek burned and his knuckles ached.

"Listen, we're here to help. The men are from Savalas. He wanted to scare his daughter. Only problem is one of the local men he hired heard about the map and wants it."

That caught Jack's attention. He glared at Ty. "Get them the fuck off me. I'll see to Kat and then we'll talk." Whoever that local was, he would die, but first Kat needed him.

She looked so tiny sprawled at the feet of The Circle's finest. *Stupid asses.*

"Ahh," she groaned and cupped her nose.

"Oh, baby, I'm so sorry that happened. If I had known I would've warned you." He ran his hands over her shoulders and down her arms, then over her ribs, hips and legs. Nothing appeared broken, except her nose. Her pretty little nose.

Her eyes cut over to him. Already, a bluish tint darkened below her left one. What bothered him more was the hurt shining out of them. No chance then that she'd been out and hadn't heard what had been said.

"I can explain—"

"Get away from me." She struggled to sit up. He reached out, and she jerked away, glaring with heated anger. She looked around and stomped her foot. "Don't touch me. You're no better than my dad, using me for your own means. I should've listened to him. Where's my gun?"

"Sugar, let me explain." He resisted the urge to pull her into his arms. One thing he knew about strong women, they hated being coddled when they were pissed.

She raised her hand and shook her head.

Okay. No explanations yet.

Standing back, but staying nearby in case she lost her balance, he waited until she reached her feet before turning to Ty. From the smile on the man's face, he enjoyed Jack's predicament too much.

Jack stepped toward the asshole.

"Katerina, you better tell him." Ty crossed his arms and raised an eyebrow.

A chill washed over him. Jack turned in time to see her shaking her head as he asked, "What the hell is he talking about?"

"Like you said, he's a big asshole that doesn't know when to shut his big stupid mouth. I want my gun back!"

He never claimed to be a genius, but he'd always considered himself streetwise and character savvy. He was cynical enough to catch people in their lies. No way would Katerina Savalas...

Her wary expression told him more than she probably wanted.

Cornering her between the wall and a shelf, without touching, he towered over her, wishing she'd try to escape.

The final straw before tossing her over his shoulder and spanking her ass. "Your dad. He put you up to this." It was becoming clear. "And what part did Ty play in this? How long have you two been in this together?"

"Talk about not having faith in the one you love," she mumbled.

Love? She loved him? Sad state of affairs when he couldn't remember the last woman to say it to his face. Marie had told him before but only as friends. She was such a pushover. Look at who she married. Ryker was a mean son-of-a-bitch, and she was crazy about him.

With his chest knotted up, he pulled back his head and narrowed his eyes. "What do you mean?"

"Ty and I have known each other for a few years. On occasion, we work for Daddy by going undercover as a redneck couple. Most people ignore us, thinking we're stupid and harmless, but we always come back with the information Daddy needs. That's why he knew where to find the door." She glared at Ty. "Dumbass. I want my gun."

Ty shook his head and ignored her, keeping his attention on Jack.

Jack began to relax. Was that all? Those big brown eyes looked up and he felt like melting at her feet. Beneath one eye, a crescent had already darkened to a deep purple. Her swollen nose had to ache. Poor baby. He'd talk to her later about why she thought it important to hide the fact she knew Ty.

He leaned down, almost nose to nose. "What did you mean about the one you love?" Those dark eyes softened as she looked into his.

Aw, hell! She loved him. What a relief! The love he felt for her had started from the first time he saw her tied up in that wack-a-doodle's cabin in Gatlinburg. Bruised and scratched, she'd been ready to fight anyone who touched her.

Without a care of who watched, he kissed her, wanting to possess every inch of her. He hauled her up by the waist and then flattened her to the wall. She wrapped her arms and legs around him.

"I love a porn show as much as the next guy. So I hate to break up this little love-fest, but I have good news, bad news." Ty edged around and his other men spread out. "The good news is the map is real."

"Of course, it's real." Kat looked at Jack then Ty. Her gaze returned to the man holding her. "I swear it's real. Go look at it. It's sitting on my bed."

Jack considered himself to be a good liar. In his business, it came in handy to persuade people to do what he wanted. But he wanted to tell the truth to Kat. He wanted their relationship to start over with a clean slate.

"Sorry, baby, I don't know what Ty is trying to pull, but it isn't."

At that moment, the lights in the basement came on and several men poured down the steps. Jack shoved her toward the wall and stepped around, putting his body in the line of fire. Instead of attacking, they joined Ty's men pointing their guns at Jack. What had happened to Savalas's men?

But one man he recognized.

Jack asked, "Lonnie, what the hell are you doing here?"

The big man grinned, flashing a diamond stud embedded in a front tooth. The tattoo on the side of his face wrinkled. "I owe that bitch a whole lot of pain. She'll never kick another man in the balls again."

"That's the voice! He wore a black mask and chased me out into the woods," said Kat. She started toward Lonnie, but Jack grabbed her around the waist and tossed her behind him.

"Is that right?" Ty asked before Jack had a chance.

"The stupid bitch busted me in the balls. She owes me." Lonnie nervously looked from Ty to Jack.

"That's what any creep deserves." Kat reached around as if she wanted to scratch the man's eyes out.

"Damn it to hell! Stay put!" Jack grabbed her arm and shook his head. Heaven help him around women who had more guts than sense.

Lonnie waved his gun toward Kat. "I wanted to try out a little of what Jack's been getting. Only fair, seeing as he's been getting it on with mine. Everyone knows he likes other men's old ladies."

What the hell?

"I never touched your wife, you fucking idiot. You were there the whole time." Were they all insane?

"Enough!" Ty stalked over to Lonnie.

The big man's eyes widened, and he lifted his gun.

Ty shot him between the eyes.

Kat screamed.

"What the fuck was that for?" Jack stared at the friend he didn't know anymore. Something was terribly wrong and he needed to know the answer. "What's with all the armed men?"

Ty wiped at his face, smearing the blowback.

"Jack, Jack, Jack. You have to understand that while you've been holed up in the wilds of Alabama, your beloved organization has been under attack." He pulled his shirttail from his pants and cleaned his face. "I warned Theo when he threw me into his prison that I would find a way to take everything he loved from him."

"Ryker killed Theo."

"Funny thing about that. Ryker, that ugly scarred bastard, is just as guilty. He hunted me down and handed me over to Theo. He deserves everything I planned to do to that psycho before he cheated me. The money I can get from the gold will help me take it all over."

"So the fake map is actually real. But Ryker had no part of my assignment."

"Right on both counts, my friend."

Hell, no. He wasn't his friend. That was already proven.

"What about Kat? What's her part in it?" Jack reached behind him, ensuring that she hadn't moved.

"That's another situation."

An accented voice came from the shadows of the secret entrance. "My daughter had her part to play. I knew she had a special interest in you. If I asked her to bring you into this, she'd keep you busy. We had a lot of work to do with the real map." Mikolas Savalas stepped out of shadows and stopped beside Ty.

"The real map?" Kat moved next to Jack. He wrapped an arm around her shoulders. Her body trembled from anger or fear, he wasn't sure.

"After the first break-in we switched it out with a fake one. We've already located and moved the gold to a safe place, and my people have already started the process of melting and selling it off."

"If you had already taken the map from me, why the fake or the second break-in?"

Ty nodded to the body. "That wasn't part of the plan. He'd forgotten he was on a need-to-know basis. He didn't need to know we had the map already, and this was our plan to keep Jack out of the way. Only problem is Jack has his own agenda."

• • •

Katerina glanced around. Everyone's focus was on her father.

Men were fucking crazy! Ty, her dad and Jack had all lied to her. They had lied to each other. Hers was nothing more than omitting a fact. She hadn't been sure how Jack would react if he knew she and Ty had a past. In fact, Ty had been the one her father had wanted her to marry. His new partner.

What had she done to deserve this treatment? She'd wanted to be independent. Live life the way she wanted. She'd thought Jack had understood. She'd thought he might be falling in love with her as much as she loved him. That was the trap. It was a woman's nature to want to please the one who protected her. She in turn would take care of him, comfort him.

Oh, my God! She did love the poetry-spouting, cat-loving he-man.

One more glance confirmed no one really was looking at her and Jack. She pulled on his arm, hoping he would follow quickly before anyone realized what they were doing. Instead, Jack shoved her toward the exit and jumped the man nearest the doorway. Without waiting to see if Jack was behind her, she ran down the tracks, concentrating on not tripping on the railroad ties. The light from the basement illuminated enough of the tunnel for her to see the end and a brighter light. She prayed that Ty hadn't thought to post someone there. As she ran into the garage an explosion of gunfire echoed behind her. She stopped and turned. Jack.

No. No. No!

Before she could take a step, arms wrapped around her and picked her up. The man slammed her against his chest, squeezing so she couldn't catch her breath. Then just as quickly his hold loosened and a large hand covered her mouth before she recovered and screamed. Terrified, she tried to look up at her captor. Was he another of Ty's men? She struggled. Then a man with horrific scars on one side of his face walked in front of her. Ryker, the commander of The Circle. The man frightened her more than she cared to admit.

"Katerina, we're here to help Jack." The gravelly voice wasn't reassuring. At this point, she wasn't sure if she could trust anyone. As if he read her mind, he nodded at the giant holding her. "Let her go."

As her toes touched the floor, she quickly put some space between her and her attacker. Gasping for air, she turned and glanced up at the man. He looked familiar. It was something about that stubborn chin and the V-shaped scar on his cheek.

"Rex?"

"Yep." He studied her as much as she looked him over.

She pointed to the exit. "What are you waiting for? Didn't you hear the gunfire? He might be bleeding and face first on the floor." Her feet dug in to run back the way she came. What could she say? Love was never logical. Despite having no gun, and who knew when or where she'd dropped her knife, she was determined to save Jack.

Rex grabbed the back of her shirt and hauled her back to face Ryker.

"Knowing Jack, he'll come out of this smelling like roses," Rex said in a snarky tone.

"If you're not going to help, why are you here?" She glared long and hard at Rex. From what Jack had told her, he and Ryker had no love lost between them. But brothers had to be a different thing. Her brothers would die for each other and her, despite their bullying ways.

"A favor to a friend," said Rex as he nodded toward Ryker.

"Is this how you treat your brother? After all he's done for you?" She looked at the huge guy with a cold stare. "You should be thankful."

The confused, angry look explained a lot.

"You don't know?" When Rex frowned and remained quiet, she explained. "Your drunk asshole of a father had beaten your mom to death and Jack showed the man how it felt. Your dad didn't get up and leave you two. Jack did what he needed to do to protect you, his younger brother, from an abusive lunatic. He loves you that much. He's risked his life several times trying to make up for it. You need to remember that and one more thing. He was an abused kid too. And when he gave you that scar, he knew something had to change.

"And have you ever wondered why he shaves his head?" When Rex merely stared at her, she said, "I asked. I had a feeling it wasn't to hide a receding hairline or to make a fashion statement. He hated looking in the mirror and seeing his dad. Your dad. He said you look like your mom and her side of the family. He looked like the man he hated and killed to protect you."

Rex studied her for several seconds and finally said, "Okay. Let's go and see what we can do to save that paragon of truth and righteousness." Though Rex said it sarcastically, he looked less resentful of saving his brother. Something had clicked in the big guy's brain.

Chapter Nine

Jack wanted to throw up. His head pounded like a meat cleaver on cube steak, and he had no doubt that his brain had been well tenderized.

With one eye open, he checked out the situation. In shock, his eyes opened and stared straight into the unblinking black eyes of a white cat wearing a pink bow. How in the hell had he turned up in Kat's bed?

He struggled to sit up in the soft bed, but his body screamed in protest from what felt like a couple broken ribs and numerous bruises. Then it all came back to him. Ty. Mikolas. Being beaten and then flashes of light, echoing gunfire and lots of feet running by his prone body. He remembered a woman crying. Kat? Where the hell was she?

Taking it inch by inch, he slid toward the edge of the bed. Movement at the bottom of the bed caused him to jump.

Damn it! He clutched at his side. He was wrapped tight as an Egyptian mummy.

"Scared the shit out of me, Kinky." Jack glared at the

feline. She high-stepped it over the covers and meowed, rubbing against his bare thigh before jumping off the bed.

Looking down, Jack lifted the sheet. Not a stitch on if he didn't count the beige bandages around his torso.

"What are you doing up?" Kat walked into the bedroom, shaking a finger at him.

"The bruises on my ribs tell me I didn't dream it." He looked at her from the corner of his eyes. "Or did I, and this is from the time your brothers tried to squash me flat by piling on top of me? Did I dream all the other stuff?"

"It's all up to you and what kind of stuff you're talking about. If you're talking about how my dad and Ty betrayed and tried their best to kill you, then no. You didn't dream it."

"So we did make love, and I told you how I felt." Most of it slammed into his mind. He ignored all the pain, as he watched the woman he wanted so desperately. He didn't give a damn about the betrayals or what The Circle had planned for him. He was through with it all. That was, if this woman would have him.

"How do you feel, Jack?" She eased up to the bed, running her hand over his shaved head.

He closed his eyes and sighed with a long purr.

"You've been around your cat too much," she teased.

"Ah, sugar, you have a magical touch, what can I say?"

She leaned down and kissed him on the lips. Nothing hot and heavy, just a teasing reminder of what she tasted like.

"Tell me," she pressed.

"I love you, Katerina Savalas." He ignored the pain as he reached and brought her into his lap. *"If music be the food of love, play on."*

"Shakespeare. Oh, Jack. I do love you," she whispered in his ear and nipped at the lobe.

"I hate to interrupt you two...whatever." Rex stepped into the room, looking around with alarm at the numerous Hello Kitty dolls. "What the fuck?"

"Same thing I said." Jack grinned.

"Hush. They're mine and I love them."

Kat struggled to stand, and Jack held on as he raised his chin. "Rex."

"Brother." Rex lifted his chin in return greeting and remained in the doorway.

Brother? He'd thought to never hear Rex call him that again.

"What are you doing here?" Jack had a suspicion, but wanted to hear it from his only living relative.

"Saving your worthless ass. Again."

"Say something," Katerina said and pinched one male nipple.

"What do you want me to say?" Jack leaned away and rubbed the offended piece of flesh.

"Thank you would be nice." For goodness sakes, the man needed lessons in humility. Then she felt his body tense, not from pain this time, and from the look in his eyes, he had come to a place in his life he was unsure what to say next.

"You really didn't give me a chance," he murmured.

He cleared his throat.

"Thanks, Rex. I'm surprised." Katerina brushed the back of her knuckles down his swollen cheekbone. Jack continued, "But I really appreciate it. I don't want to think what would've happened to Kat, if you guys hadn't come in when you did."

"You have her to thank that we did. When Ryker got the call last night, he was a little wary of it being a setup."

The confused look on his face when Jack turned to her, made her a little nervous.

"How did you know we would need help?"

"I didn't." She felt her face warm. "I wanted Ryker to give me Rex's number. We talked a little. Even before you told me what you did last night, I knew it bothered you that you two were on the outs. Everyone needs family. Blood or those you choose. I never imagined it to be perfect timing."

She leaned down and kissed him, taking her time, letting him know how important he was to her.

"We can talk later." Rex's deep voice pulled her away from what they had started. In front of a guest no less. Her face flushed again.

"I'll be down in a couple hours. Will you be there?"

Rex hesitated and then said, "Yeah. Ryker's questioning some of the men. Ty has to be hiding somewhere nearby. He should be running out of his nine lives soon." The big guy looked around and shook his head. "He let your dad go with a promise to cooperate on future missions."

Katerina felt a little guilty for not asking but she knew her dad could worm his way out of anything. She would call her brothers later and fill them in. They deserved to know what their dad had been up to.

"Thanks." She nodded and smiled at Rex.

When the door closed, she clasped his face and looked deep into his eyes. "Mr. Jack Drago, will you marry me?"

"I thought it was the man's place to ask the woman."

She grinned and waited.

"Who am I to argue? Yeah. I'll marry you." He smiled and then kissed her.

Afraid of hurting him, she moved her hands from his face and wrapped her arms around his neck.

When they stopped to draw breath, she pushed back, tilting her head to examine his face. "You need to hurry and get well. I have a feeling you're real handy with a brush and roller."

She laughed when he narrowed his eyes.

"That's why you're marrying me. I can reach the high places and lift heavy objects."

Laughing, she massaged his biceps. "Those muscles need to be put to use as they're intended."

"Oh, I can show you how handy they can be."

"I bet you can."

She nudged him back until he was stretched out beneath her. "I'll be gentle. I promise," she teased.

He shivered when her tongue swiped across his collarbone.

"Yes, ma'am."

Kidnapped For A Day

Short Story

Chapter One

"Shut up." The voice bellowed from the shadows of the Sandbox Bar and Grill's parking lot followed by the sound of flesh hitting flesh.

A distinct feminine whimper penetrated the predawn morning silence.

Luke Warren's orders were to wait until Emma Cooper got off work at two and then *try to save* her from the staged attack by one of his men. Physical violence had no part of the act. Since he'd seen the other three waitresses leave minutes earlier, that left only her.

He growled in frustration beneath his breath. They had been instructed to go easy on her. The idiot was to frighten her, not mistreat her. Taking a second to control his temper, he marched around the corner, preparing to play his part. His boss knew how he felt about mistreating women.

For Christ's sake, he had two sisters he loved and never wanted them involved in his life. Thankfully, his sisters had enough sense to stay home and snuggle with their spouses in the safety of their soft beds. Their lives were so different from the way he lived his. However, recently his life had brushed up against his youngest sister's best friend, Emma. All because of her brother's clandestine life.

Another slap pierced the air before he located them.

A huge shadow moved beneath a busted security light. Luke stopped and watched as the mass separated and took shape. The man loomed over a much smaller, curvy silhouette as he squeezed her upper arm. The feminine form covered her head with her free arm in a protective stance.

The man wasn't part of his operation.

With practiced ease, Luke palmed his Glock 43 from the holster in his boot. As he double-fisted it, he edged around a truck and halted.

Scrutinizing the man, Luke noted he hadn't pulled out a gun. So he slipped his weapon back into his boot. No need to escalate the situation with the threat of gunfire. A good, old-fashioned fist fight was what he needed. As the bastard raised his hand to strike Emma again, Luke darted forward and slammed into the man's torso. With a grunt he landed on top and the man's head hit the asphalt with a hollow *thunk* and then the asshole remained motionless.

Luke recognized the thug belonging to Mikolas Savalas, a crime lord out of Atlanta. Where the hell was his guy?

A sick feeling swirled in his stomach. His employer had warned him Savalas and his people could be sniffing around. They were a tricky bunch, who would do anything to get one over on The Circle, the private military organization Luke worked for.

He pressed two fingers to the side of the unconscious man's throat. Relieved to feel a steady pulse, Luke slipped out a roll of Velcro zip ties from one pocket and nylon zip ties from the other, then flipped the unconscious man onto his stomach. Most people would think it strange he always carried a supply, but in his line of business being prepared could mean the difference between life or death. Anyway, they didn't take up a lot of room. He made quick work of entwining the ties around the man's wrists and ankles, effectively hogtying him. By the time the unconscious man woke and worked them off, Luke should be long gone.

Luke rose to his feet and turned toward the woman.

Cupping the side of her face, she grimaced and stared wide-eyed at the thug. "Is he dead?"

A few seconds ticked by before he realized he was staring. He blamed it on the beer he'd downed before leaving the bar and the early hour of the morning. He'd forgotten about her beautiful eyes.

"Emma." Time to put on his tarnished white knight armor and play the gruff hero. "What the hell are you doing in this side of Sand City?" All part of the act.

Luke's gaze traveled with consternation over the petite brunette with one cheek slightly swollen, but not as bad as he expected. He lightly brushed his knuckles across the forming bruise.

"I work here." Her voice wobbled.

"Don't you know better than to walk out alone at this time of night?" Guilt sent a chill through him. The bartender had been paid to stay behind.

Emma opened her mouth to reply, but when her gaze lifted, her eyes widened, focusing on a point past his shoulder. She gasped. He pulled his gun, and began to swing around, but a flash of light sent him to his knees followed by massive pain as blackness closed around him.

Luke lifted a hand to rub at the pulsating ache at the back of his skull. He jumped when a jingling waterfall of chain slapped his face. Squinting, he gingerly turned his head to glare at the restraint. Oh, hell. A thick manacle encircled his wrist. Welded to possibly three feet of chain, it was attached to the cot's rail, and likely the legs were bolted to the cement floor.

Thick, humid air filled his lungs as he gasped for breath, panic mounting with each second.

No, not again, he silently screamed. Using all of his concentration to regain control from past traumatic memories, he inhaled and exhaled. Inhaled. Exhaled. Over and over. He slowed each exhale to quell the initial panic. He knew the cell well. Each crack he'd counted many times. The metal door's window was too small to crawl through even if the rusty bars were brittle enough to crumble away. Buzzing fluorescent tubes from the hallway provided the only light. He'd spent eleven hellish months wasting away in the square cement block space.

Whose joke was it placing him there? He would break their neck. If not for the knowledge that The Circle organization had taken control of the former Savalas compound after his escape, he would be freaking out. The obvious reason his confidence held was that he still wore clothes. Savalas loved stripping his captives.

As he regained his composure, blinking away the grit and hated past, he checked out the rest of the cell. The only change was the figure huddled in the corner. *Damn it.* What had they done to her while he'd been out? Sure, they needed to make it look realistic, but why knock him out? And what was up with the chains? And bringing him back to this place?

"Emma," he croaked. He cleared his throat, then tried again. "Emma."

She lifted her head, revealing dark half-moon smudges

beneath her eyes from smeared makeup and lack of sleep. Bruises and tear-streaked cheeks finished the pitiful picture, but she raised her chin, pulling herself together.

Good. The woman had guts, but he hated seeing the bruises.

That wasn't to happen.

Then he spotted the metal collar. Cursing beneath his breath, he sat up, clutching his own chain. The assholes went too far. He was well aware his organization would execute any abuse to get the information needed. But did they not understand how delicate the woman was?

"Who else hit you? Did they touch..." He stopped his line of questioning when she dropped her face into her hands and shook her head, sobs racking her body. He was an idiot. She didn't need his interrogation.

Curling his fingers, he hoped he could resist punching the next person to show his face.

The few times he'd been around Emma, she'd been quiet, modest, polite, and sweet. No one with her innocence should be pulled into the middle of the craziness he dealt with more often than he wanted to think about. Sure, time was limited, and experience had taught his organization that by placing someone in an unusual, harrowing situation, the person would promise a first born in exchange to return to their everyday safe life. Still, she hadn't deserved to be treated so cruelly.

Glancing her way again, he squeezed his hands into fists. Desire to caress her cheek and ease her worries tightened his chest, but she needed to stay anxious. Otherwise, he would be defeating the purpose of the mission. But he guaranteed they'd never touch her again. Clanging brought him back to his situation. *Damn chain.* He yanked at it and waited, giving her time to manage her feelings as he passed the time imagining ways to tear apart the person who moved from intimidating to terrorizing an innocent.

After a few moments, her weeping slowed. Then she wiped away her tears with a torn sleeve.

"I-I don't know. I mean they shoved me into a big SUV, bruising my arms, hip." She rubbed her right side. "But they didn't try, you know." She blushed, and dipped her head as she pulled at the collar with a trembling hand. After a couple of minutes, she gave up the effort to rid herself of the collar and eased to her feet, swaying, causing the chain connected to her collar to jingle.

"Be careful or you'll faint. I can't help you from here." He shook his manacle as he scooted across the cot until his back rested against the wall. "Come, sit here, if your chain reaches this far. Go slow. Don't want you to fall." His voice maintained an even tone in an effort to lull her to trust him. "Take it slower."

She slid one foot and then another while grasping the chain. When she reached the cot, she became tangled and landed half on, half off the thin mattress.

He reached for her, but came up short. *Stupid ass chain.* How many more bruises could the woman endure? "Are you all right?"

Rubbing at her left hip, she pulled herself up until she also sat leaning against the wall, a few inches separating them.

"I'm a little clumsy but okay. Nothing like matching bruises." Her eyes welled up and spilled over though she remained quiet. She blinked away the tears. "Sorry. I can't seem to stop crying."

Unable to resist any longer, he moved as far as his manacled left hand allowed and placed his free arm around her shoulders, squeezing her to his side.

"I know this looks…"he glanced around as a chill raced down his spine"bad, but I swear we'll get out of this and soon." The tremors from her body almost matched the pulsating pain in his head and neck.

Hell, she didn't deserve to be in the current screwed-up mess.

Without even thinking about it, he kissed the top of her head. Surprise washed over his torso. He wasn't the sort of guy to cuddle, not even with his sisters, but she brought out his protective side times two.

It didn't make sense. She wasn't his type.

He preferred tall, slender blondes. Emma was the total opposite, but strangely, her height-challenged frame suited his perfectly. Having her soft, rounded body tucked into his felt so right.

She sighed and leaned harder into his side, her head resting on his chest.

"What do they want with us?" She sounded like a lost, little girl, her eyes wide to the point they looked as if they might pop out.

"It's not you. It's me. I escaped and they wanted me back." His eyes closed for a few seconds in frustration. All the lies driven by the necessary setup felt so wrong, but his story had to make her feel responsible for his current predicament. It was part of the job. He needed her scared, just not to the point of being petrified. "You got caught in the middle."

"Why take me? Why me?"

He stared down into her sweet face. What was one more lie?

"They'll release you when they come back to question me."

Her gaze searched his face. She wouldn't be able to read

anything he didn't want her to. He'd been told many times he was a good liar. That he could make a fortune playing poker. Yet, he never gambled. Why should he? He gambled with his life on every mission.

Unable to resist it any longer, he leaned down and swiped a thumb over one tear-stained cheek and then the other. The silkiness of her skin triggered his cock to harden, lengthen. Hell, the last thing he needed was having her feeling awkward, but he could stop his response to her nearness as much as he could stop his hands from moving. As in, not at all. He appreciated the silkiness of her skin beneath his fingertips as they traveled down her neck and across her collarbone. His strokes wandered along her arms, over her soft curves until he stopped at her thighs, hovering over where her legs joined.

Though her tremors stopped, her face changed to a pretty pink. Her eyelids drifted half closed. She enjoyed his touch as much as he enjoyed touching her. No fear shimmered from the depths of her warm eyes. Her lips parted with a sigh.

Damn, those kissable lips.

Admittedly, he'd noticed her full lower lip before. Perfectly suckable. But moving around, working dangerous assignments, and keeping his business private from his only family necessitated he ignore his desire for the sprite in his arms. So difficult to stay away. Especially as she was his sister's best friend. What was the chance of him finding another one like her? She'd never want anything to do with him after she survived their ordeal. Just his luck.

He groaned and bounced his head against the wall. They'd loosened something in his brain when they hit him. That had to be why he acted so maudlin.

Chapter Two

Emma melted against Luke. Really, how many women could resist snuggling up to a broad-shouldered, long-legged man with such inscrutable gray eyes? She certainly couldn't. She barely managed to stay away from him even with his sisters' warnings of Luke being a heartbreaker.

Besides, he always looked at her with politeness. Well, until he woke up in a cell with her.

She rested her head beneath his chin and closed her eyes, soaking in the comfort he offered. As his hands roamed over her, she struggled to keep her breathing even despite the rapid beat of her heart. When he hesitated at her upper thighs, she swallowed a gasp. Her surroundings disappeared as every nerve in her body centered between her legs.

The clank of metal hitting metal down the hallway and a whiff of fresh air warned that someone was coming. She snapped out of the lust-induced trance his touch had created.

Luke's massive body stiffened beneath her.

In response, she started to tremble again, but he quickly

wrapped a muscular arm around her waist and squeezed tight in a mixture of warning and protection, dragging her onto his lap. A calmness came over her. From the tidbits told by his sister about his interest in martial arts, he was capable of handling any frightening situation.

His chain rattled.

How could he fight with one hand hampered?

Unhurried heavy footsteps approached from down the hallway.

Part of her wanted to move away from Luke before their captor came to the cell. Yet, deep inside, she wanted to remain in his embrace. Safely tucked against his warm body. She reasoned even an independent, confident woman like herself loved a strong man willing to protect her.

Then again, how embarrassing being caught embracing while on a man's lap. And really, they had to look a total wreck, what with her bruised face and degrading collar, and Luke with blood dried from his temple to ear, matted in his hair and spattered down his light-blue T-shirt. Dirt coated a strip of his shirt and on down one side of his jeans. Probably left over from when he attacked the asshole who had hit her. She didn't want to think of how she smelled. The cell's human waste stench was bad enough and probably had already seeped into her pores.

Maybe she should move. She closed her eyes, incapable of making a decision at that point as she continued to soak in his comforting touch. What did it really matter?

The weak light in the cell dimmed even more as someone partially blocked the small, barred opening in the door.

"Welcome back, asshole," the deep voice said.

She made out only a silhouette of a perfectly shaped bald head. Not many men were lucky enough to have one.

Then white teeth appeared, like the Cheshire Cat, almost glowing in the low light. Shudders ran down her body.

Goodness, she was going off her rocker. Who cared about the shape of his head or how shiny his teeth? She warily eyed the man.

"Where's Savalas? I expected his greasy ass." Luke lightly squeezed her waist as he used a threatening tone.

Was he telling her he would do his best to protect her and she needed to be quiet and play along? Not that she was a mind reader, but he had tried to save her from the attacker. His sisters swore he had a white knight syndrome.

Thank goodness.

Syndrome or not, she allowed herself to relax against his hard, virile body. She'd never experienced having someone willingly place themselves between her and danger. Yeah, she had loving parents and a solicitous brother, but she didn't remember anyone actually protecting her. No one had ever acted worried about her well-being.

"He's busy. He sent me to take out the trash." He leaned back from the opening. Then she heard a beeping sound as if he'd punched a code into a keypad.

The door swung open, allowing more light to pour through as the man stepped inside. His head nearly brushed the top of the metal door frame. Baby-blue eyes appeared to glow, not with a fanatical shine, but more with total amusement at the situation. He hung back enough to keep more than chain length away.

"Considering I was gone and then you brought me back, that's all on you, asshole," Luke said, each word coated with scorn.

Why was Luke provoking the man?

In the dim light, she narrowed her eyes to more closely examine the thug. He had piercings in one eyebrow, both earlobes, and bottom lip, and when he crossed his arms, his T-shirt stretched across defined pecs and biceps. Tattoos peeked out from around the neck and below the short sleeves, covering his forearms and hands. He was a good-looking man, but something about his tone revealed a hardness of spirit from years of disappointment.

She pressed against Luke's chest.

"Actually, we needed *you.*" The man's gaze dropped to her face.

"Me?" She squeaked. Luke was wrong.

Her head swam. She'd always wished to be brave, but when push came to shove, her backbone would cave. That moment was no different.

Why was she a coward? Her parents were kind to her growing up and her brother rarely teased her. Her family always called her a dreamer and she agreed. She loved to read anything with romance and fantasy in it. She was the ideal, helpless damsel in distress and she didn't care what other people thought. Luke certainly needed women like her so he could be a successful knight in shining armor. From everything else she'd heard from his sisters, Luke was courageous and a bit of a daredevil.

Maybe that was part of why he attracted her.

"Yes. Dickhead here got in the way. We need you to tell us where your brother is. He has something we want back."

She knew it! She loved her brother, but he constantly stirred up trouble despite promising not to involve the family in any of his shenanigans.

"Emma, tell them what they want to know. They'll let you go," Luke whispered in her ear. The scuff on his jaw lightly scraped her cheek causing her to shiver.

How did he do it? Was it the mysterious danger

surrounding him? None of the men she dated since meeting Luke had compared. He was such a man's man.

Pulling her head back, she looked into his eyes. Concern reflected in his ruggedly handsome features as his gaze met hers. He'd proven he would protect her, but at what cost?

Returning her attention to their captor, she nodded. "I'll tell you if you release Luke first."

The man smirked.

"What the hell?" Luke shook his head. "No. That's not going to happen, Emma. They don't bargain." He cupped her cheek with a big hand as his gaze met hers. "I appreciate the gesture, but don't worry about me. Do as he says. That's the quickest way to return home."

"No. If they want information from me, they need to agree." Where was her nerve coming from? She appreciated his concern. Scared silly, she somehow kept her voice steady despite how much her body shook.

The man shifted in the doorway and cleared his throat. "He's right. No negotiation. I'll give you two hours to hash it out. When I return, you'd better be cooperative." The clank of the door closing brought a mix of relief and dread.

"Look at me, girl." Luke's voice colored each word with sadness and desperation. "These people aren't messing around. You have to cooperate and quickly. The next time he asks, tell him or they will make you, and you don't want to go there. I'll take care of myself. Remember, I escaped their clutches before."

"Then I'll escape with you." What was coming out of her mouth? Obviously, being in his arms made her daring. Maybe she had a little of her brother's spirit in her.

"Emma—" He stopped talking, stared into her eyes for a

moment. Then he covered her mouth with his. Tongues tangled and stroked. Heat coated her from head to toes.

Wow. She'd never been kissed so thoroughly.

He squeezed her tight like she was about to slip out of his hold. Such a wonderful sensation. He kissed as if she could provide their last breath. Her hands caressed his chest and shoulders as if they had a will of their own. Threading her fingers into his hair, she sucked on his lower lip. His groan vibrated through her. Short of breath, she let go and leaned back.

"Sorry. Did I hurt you?"

He chuckled. "No, baby. But you're so much more than I ever imagined."

"Yeah?"

"Oh, yeah." He leaned his forehead against hers. "But this isn't the time or place."

"I—" She nipped at his swollen lower lip. Never had she ever acted so daring, but the fullness tempted her to take another taste. "I guess I could lie about where my brother is."

"No. Don't lie. They'll check before releasing you. If they don't spot him, they won't be as nice the second time they ask."

With a tilt of her head, she narrowed her eyes. "You're a lot like my brother."

"I'm not sure I like being compared to your brother after that kiss."

She giggled and covered her mouth. Where did that come from? She wasn't the type to giggle. Laugh, yes; giggle, no. After a sigh, she said, "He's not very forthcoming with his life. I know he travels all around the world, but never brings back pictures or fun stories like everyone else. Your sister and I have talked about how much you two have in common. Except I think you lied to your family about your destinations, unlike my brother. He knows I don't have anyone if something happens to him. So he makes sure to leave a note with his contact info."

A strange expression crossed his face.

"What's wrong?" She placed a hand on his shoulder. Did he feel bad about how he treated his sisters' anxiety?

Using one finger, he slid it across her brow, brushing strands of hair out of the way. An innocent touch, but such a turn on.

"Nothing. I think your brother is lucky to have a sweet sister like you, and I think you've proven you can tolerate bad situations."

She smiled. "True. Despite what he thinks."

"Let's get comfortable and talk some more." He shifted to lean his back against the wall. Her arms automatically circled his waist and her cheek landed over his heart. A tugging on her hair surprised her. He carefully untangled her hair with his fingers. "I'm not about to let you get hurt again." His voice rumbled beneath her ear.

"I guess you'll need to get us out of here."

His chest rose and fell with a frustrated sigh. "No. It took me eleven months last time. They'd have that exit covered. Besides, I need you safe before I try anything."

She pushed away and slipped off his lap to sit next to him. A feeling like a fist squeezing her heart sent panic racing through her. How could she choose? "So I have to pick between you or my brother?"

He lifted up her hand. "No. Between *you* and your brother. I don't count in this scenario." The press of his lips against her palm caused a wonderful tingling to shoot up her arm. "Please, baby. You don't understand how much danger you're in. Think about it. We have a little time. Here."

He placed her hand on his chest and she leaned against his shoulder. Solid and safe. That was Luke Warren. His sisters loved him dearly. She understood why. He would be easy to fall in love with, but like her brother, trusting and loving someone else besides family would be difficult for him.

She knew he was right, but her brother was the only person alive who loved her. How could she betray him?

Chapter Three

Luke covered her hand with his, waiting for her decision.

Scum of the earth. Yep, that was him.

Probably an hour had passed as they leaned against each other and listened to each other breathe. Time was running out. She had no business being there.

"Your sisters are going to worry about you if they let me go and not you." Her eyes glistened in the dim lighting. Her voice was husky with emotion.

Please don't cry. I'm not worth it. "They'll be okay. They believe I have an out-of-country assignment. It usually keeps me out of touch for six months."

"What is it you do?"

"If I told you, I'd have to kill you." Not quite true, but she reacted like so many other people did, assuming he was teasing.

She sat up and slapped his arm. "That's horrible. Quit kidding. Your sister said you're involved with consulting work, but she never said what type."

"I consult on military weapons training."

"That sounds almost sinister."

With a shrug, he used the momentum to put his arm around her and pull her in tighter, returning her head to rest on his chest again. She felt good there. It was like his soul had found his better half. Her sweetness helped to comfort him. The brightness shining out of her eyes shoved all of the horrible things he'd seen and done back into the dark recesses of his mind.

"Strangely, normal." The lie came out too easily. He rubbed his cheek across the top of her head. "The meetings are often set at really nice resorts. I've never been the type to take pictures of the places. That's why my sisters don't believe me. Does your brother send pictures?"

"Nah. But since I knew he was working, I never thought to ask. Besides, I never look at the notes he sends me, but he always returns around the date he told me before he left." She yawned. Considering what her body had been through and the inactivity for the last hour, the strain was catching up with her. "I wish I had a book to read."

"So you're saying I'm boring?"

"No. Just the last book my brother sent me started off really good," she mumbled.

He tensed at her comment. "He sends you books often?"

"Huh? No. Uh, it's kind of rare for him to do that." Her voice drifted off on the last word.

She was lying. That had to be the way he contacted her. Maybe if he got her mind on something else.

"I love to read, too. Usually westerns. What type of books do you like to read?"

"Anything with romance and fantasy." She softened against his body.

They talked for several more minutes before their jailer

showed up with enough noise to wake the dead, the door swung open with a final clank, and the big guy walked in.

"Hello, lovebirds. Anyone want to live another day?"

She gasped and began to shake again. *Damn it.*

Why couldn't Jack Drago show up a little later? He wanted to confirm what he'd guessed. He glared at his accomplice. They had worked a few missions together and normally got along, but the big guy persisted in rubbing him the wrong way in their current assignment.

Luke hauled her onto his lap and wrapped an arm across her chest to her opposite shoulder.

"Check the book on the nightstand at her house on Swan Street," Luke said, as he tightened his hold and covered her mouth with his other hand. "It should be a romantic fantasy. A sealed note should be in it with his address." About halfway through his betrayal and her squealing, she bit his hand. He hissed with pain, but finished providing the information. It had to be done. The Circle was known for mercilessness. No way would he allow anyone to hurt her.

Jack nodded. "Shouldn't take us long to pick it up. We'll likely know where the asshole is before nightfall. If the info is right, she'll be released then."

Emma began to wail louder, still muffled by his hand. Then she wiggled, trying to break free without much luck as she was stymied by his constraining embrace.

Luke lifted his chin in understanding. He waited until Jack left before freeing her.

She continued her attack but with more vigor, striking his arms and stomach as she proceeded to talk about his parentage. Ignoring her to check on his hand—the hits were no more than playful thumps—he was relieved to see no blood. The little vixen. Then she slapped his face. Hard.

The woman had a healthy swing. He clasped her wrist as another slap came at him again.

"Enough, Emma." Almost nose-to-nose, he enunciated each word carefully. "I understand you're mad, but I told you I wouldn't let anyone hurt you. Giving them the information will prevent that. I feel certain your brother can take care of himself." He dropped her arm and tensed, expecting her to hit him once again.

She scrambled to her feet. The chinking of the chain hanging from her collar irritated the hell out of him. Why hadn't he insisted on the asshole removing it? They should've never placed it around that delicate neck in the first place. The prick had done it to intimidate her. An overkill in his opinion.

Scooting to the edge of the cot, he tested the position of the chain attached to his hand. As he guessed, unless he wanted to stand with one shoulder down, he might as well stay seated. Feet on the floor and the back of his knees against the edge of the cot, he spread his legs and patted the mattress between them.

"Come here, baby. Nothing will be solved by you standing there. It's hours before dusk." The sadness on her face almost had him telling her everything would be okay. But how could he promise her that? Who could really predict the future?

"I should've never trusted you." She grimaced.

He held out his free hand, palm up. "Please. Let me hold you."

"You're a real bastard, you know that?"

"Yeah. You're not the first to say that. But I need you in my arms. I'm afraid." Afraid she would never let him hold her again. If The Circle killed her brother, she'd never forgive him. He couldn't lose her.

She blinked and opened her mouth to respond but nothing came out.

His statement had obviously surprised her. Hell, it surprised him. Many times he'd thought as much, but it was the first time he'd spoken it out loud.

Tears streamed down her face as she shuffled to the cot and crawled into his lap. They held each other with all their might for a good minute.

"You don't play fair. I'm mad at you." She sniffed, swiping her sleeve across her cheeks, and relaxed.

A deep, long sigh escaped his lips. Damn, she belonged there. He loosened his hold and leaned back against the wall, arranging her cheek to press against his sternum. She belonged in his arms, just like that.

"Sorry, baby. Your safety is important to me."

He kissed the top of her head and squeezed her as if his life depended on it. In a way, he felt like it did. He never believed a woman could take over his every thought.

Why had she affected him at that point? Why not when he'd seen her at his youngest sister's house? Was it the tears? Yes and no. He'd always hated it when his sisters cried, but it was different. She'd proven she had guts, the necessary willpower to stand up to those who threatened her.

Damn. What was he thinking to fall in love with her?

Emma woke with a start. The steady thumping beneath her ear along with the rise and fall of his chest felt so good. She closed her eyes again and immersed her senses into the moment. Just knowing the firm chest belonged to Luke Warren soothed her. Even his betrayal of her confidence couldn't destroy her feelings for the mystery man. In spite of the previous harrowing hours and how she'd come to realize he was flawed, she still wanted him.

Lifting her head, she stared into the face of the man who meant so much to her. From the dark aura surrounding him, she suspected his work was as dangerous as he was, but she was careful not to let her imagination run wild. Except at night, in bed alone. Then he'd been the lead in all of her fantasies.

The clang of metal down the hallway alerted her to their time coming to an end.

"Luke, wake up. He's back."

"I'm awake." He clasped her head and touched his forehead to hers as he whispered, "Whatever happens next be ready to run. Don't look back, don't worry about me. It's late afternoon. So run toward the sun. There's a busy strip of interstate about three miles from here. You can do it. Flag someone down and go to the nearest town. I'll make sure no one follows, but you still need to keep going forward. Remember that. Do you understand me?"

The desperation in his voice emphasized how important it was she follow his instructions. He had escaped before. He knew what to do.

"What about you, my knight?" She traced his lips. She didn't want to leave him alone. What if they killed him?

"Knight, huh?" He grabbed her hand and kissed it. "Listen to me. I'll be fine. I'm too valuable for them to kill. You need—"

"I have good news for the sweet thing." Their jailer opened the door with his usual clang.

"Take the collar off her," Luke demanded.

"All in good time." The man smirked as he took in their closeness. "But I have a couple more questions for the little firecracker. We need a little alone time." He bent down and unlocked the chain from the ring in the floor, leaving it attached to her collar.

Her skin crawled from the man's lingering leer. Obviously, he wasn't referring to alone time with Luke.

The man came nearer, slowly drawing closer by wrapping the chain around one fist. Before she knew what was happening, Luke shoved her to the side and bear-hugged the jailer, bringing them both down in a tumble of limbs onto the cot.

"Go!" Luke shouted as he head-butted the man and then hit him in the face twice.

Her collar jerked as the chain became entangled with the bodies. Then she was free. That was, she had the whole length of chain. Remembering what Luke had said, she gathered up the links and looped them around her arm. Without wasting another second, she skirted around the wrestling men and through the open doorway. Panic filled her when she heard shouting, but she somehow found the exit. No one was around. The oddness of no guards would have to be figured out later. First, she needed to escape. Then she would find a way to help Luke.

By the time she spotted the interstate, she was exhausted. Slumping behind a huge bush, she unwound the chain from her arm and wrapped it around her waist. Somehow she needed to look normal. Otherwise, no one would pick her up.

Chapter Four

Luke stood in the shadows of the open doorway and watched Emma run through the field of knee-high grass toward the interstate.

"Damn, man, why did you hit me?" Jack leaned against the door frame and fingered his jaw, a large, purple bruise quickly forming.

"It was bad enough you brought me to this hell hole and chained me, but you did the same to Emma."

"Hey, you know how the boss is. He felt the stress would heighten the realism." The bald man flashed his signature bright, devilish smile. "It worked, didn't it?"

Ignoring the question, Luke tilted his head, his gaze staying on the woman sprinting toward freedom. "Maybe I should follow her and make sure she's picked up like we planned." Rubbing his chest, he squinted as she became a dot in the distance.

"Don't worry. She'll be fine. Rick'll make sure she gets home."

"Rick. That pervert? I thought you said Katerina was doing it."

"She was sick this morning."

With Emma out of sight, he let his gaze move to Jack.

"Morning sickness?" Luke lifted his eyebrows. When they had met up to plan the mission, the big guy had mentioned they were trying for a kid.

"Yeah. Keep it to yourself. I don't need my father-in-law breathing down my neck about his first grandchild. Damn, it's going to be hell enough when he finds out." Jack tilted his head, a popping sound echoing down the empty hall-way. Then he cracked his neck in the opposite direction.

His father-in-law was the very same dangerous crime lord, Mikolas Savalas, who had captured and imprisoned Luke. Every time he thought about Jack having to deal with the man every holiday, he cringed.

Luke's gaze remained on the horizon where Emma had disappeared. "When she finds out I set her up, she's going to be pissed. Maybe I should explain." He hoped she continued to be a forgiving woman.

"You might have to get on your hands and knees and beg, if you do." Jack chuckled.

Luke nodded. "She's worth it."

Without another word, he started walking across the field. About midway, he broke into a jog. He needed to hurry. The woman was too trusting and who knew what trouble she could find herself in again.

Yeah. The last twenty-four hours had been life-altering for sure. Who would've ever guessed a bum like him would fall in love?

No denying it. She was totally worth it.

About the Author

CARLA SWAFFORD loves romance novels, action/adventure movies, and men, and her books reflect that. And on top of all that, she's crazy about hockey, and thankfully, no one has made her turn in her Southern Belle card.

So, it's no surprise she writes spicy romantic suspense filled with mercenaries, motorcycle one-percenters, and southern criminals. And in the last few years, she's included sexy hockey players in books without suspense, except for the kind that asks, how will they ever find their happily ever after?

Married to her high school sweetheart, she lives in the Southeast U.S. To find out more about Carla, be sure to visit her Facebook and TikTok pages or join her newsletter.

Website: carlaswafford.com

Also by Carla Swafford

Brothers of Mayhem Trio

Hidden Heat

Full Heat

Above currently published by Loveswept,

an imprint of Random House in ebook only

Naked Heat

The Circle Organization

Circle of Desire

Circle of Danger

Circle of Deception

Above previously published by Avon, an imprint of HarperCollins.

Circle of Dishonor (novella)

Circle of Defiance (novella

Kidnapped For A Day (short story)

Above novellas and short story available individually in Ebook and in paperback together

Atlanta Edge Hockey Romance

Crossing The Line

Fake Play

(more to come)

Southern Crime Family Trio

Jake

Sen (coming soon!)

Ethan (coming soon!)

Small-Town Duo

Loving The Small-Town Preacher's Son

Loving The Small-Town Hero

Vampire Romance

Savage Champion

www.ingramcontent.com/pod-product-compliance
Lightning Source LLC
Chambersburg PA
CBHW030754190726
48285CB00003B/845